HISTORY WAS THEIRS TO CHANGE...

It had been a joke then, but it was no longer: the South would rise again.

Dennison realized that slavery and states' rights were not the issues that concerned him. It was the preservation of the South. He just couldn't stand by and let the North win again. He could not stand by while Sherman and his bandits marched to the sea, burning everything behind them. Not when he knew every mistake that the Southern leadership would make during the war. Not when he could prevent it.

D0880212

Charter Books by Kevin Randle and Robert Cornett

REMEMBER THE ALAMO!
REMEMBER GETTYSBURG!

Ace Books by Kevin Randle and Robert Cornett

SEEDS OF WAR
THE ALDEBARAN CAMPAIGN *(coming in December)*

KEVIN RANDLE & ROBERT CORNETT

REMEMBER GETTYSBURG!

CHARTER BOOKS, NEW YORK

REMEMBER GETTYSBURG!

A Charter Book/published by arrangement with
the authors

PRINTING HISTORY
Charter edition/October 1988

All rights reserved.
Copyright © 1988 by Kevin D. Randle and Robert Charles Cornett.
This book may not be reproduced in whole or in part,
by mimeograph or any other means, without permission.
For information address: The Berkley Publishing Group,
200 Madison Avenue, New York, New York 10016.

ISBN: 1-55773-089-X

Charter Books are published by
The Berkley Publishing Group,
200 Madison Avenue, New York, New York 10016.

The name "CHARTER" and the "C" logo are trademarks belonging to
Charter Communications, Inc.

PRINTED IN THE UNITED STATES OF AMERICA

10 9 8 7 6 5 4 3 2 1

AUTHORS' NOTE: All information about Gettysburg, including the regimental designations, commanders' names and staff aides, is as accurate as possible. General Lee did have a spy by the name of Harrison, Pickett's division did manage to penetrate the Union lines, and the Union did capture an entire Confederate regiment.

ONE

Betrayed.

That's what Dr. T.R.B. Tucker felt. Betrayed by his staff who were more than just employees. Betrayed by the machinery that he had constructed himself, with the help of that staff. And betrayed by the corporation for which he worked. That, at least, was something he had expected.

He rocked back in his green leather chair, mended with electrical tape in a dozen places, and lit the white-tipped cigar that was clamped between his teeth. He tossed the burned match at an overfilled ashtray that sat amid a blizzard of paper on his old, scarred, battleship-gray desk. It went in like it had eyes.

Tucker laced his hands behind his head as he puffed up a cloud of light blue smoke and wondered what else he felt. Betrayed, yes. And disappointed, but not angry. He wasn't angry at them. Surprised that they could allow

1

themselves to be used by the corporation like that, although he didn't know what they had been offered for their help.

When he had returned, late on Sunday, all three of his assistants were gone. The power grids, the recording instruments and power settings all indicated that a rather substantial load had been sent into the past. Or a rather small load to the very distant past. Without more data, he couldn't be sure which it was. He just knew that if they had sent any humans, and then tried to retrieve them, those people were as good as dead.

For nearly an hour after his return, Tucker had checked the readings on various dials, tapes, displays, and computers. He had calculated the power expended, but without a couple of key pieces of data, he just couldn't project, accurately, what had been sent, how many loads went, or where it went.

Then he had had a shot of Beam's Choice, smoked a cigar and gone to bed. In the morning, nothing had changed. He still didn't know where his assistants were, didn't know who had been using the equipment, and didn't know what the hell was going on. He could sit and wait, as Travis had advised him when he called the corporate offices at ten, or he could spend his time trying to learn more.

Now it was nearly noon and he heard the truck used by the mailman. Tucker forced himself from his chair and walked to the door. He stopped long enough to put on his sunglasses and then stepped into the bright sunlight and the blast furnace heat. By the time he had reached the mailbox, he was sweating heavily, staining his faded cotton shirt under the arm, down the back and around the collar.

He pulled the mail from the box and returned to the lab. Once inside, he dropped the mail on the cluttered desk and walked over to the air conditioner stuck in the corner to turn it up. That done, the machine rattling and vibrating like it was about to tear itself from the wall and explode, Tucker returned to his chair.

Again, he picked up the mail and sorted through it. Although he was at a lab, financed by one of the largest oil companies in the country, he received a pile of junk mail everyday. Circulars advertizing services he didn't want, catalogs containing merchandise that he couldn't use, and suggestions about what science should be doing and wasn't. There was one envelope that caught his attention. It was bright white with ebony printing on it. The return address was a law firm in Austin and the postmark was the preceding Friday.

Tucker reached over, grabbed a screwdriver from the desk, jammed it under the flap and ripped open the envelope. Inside he found a letter, typed with a carbon ribbon on snowy bond. There was also another envelope inside, yellowed with age.

The letter said, simply, "The following was entrusted to us over a century and a half ago. We were asked to mail it on the date specified. While the request made little sense to us, the fee paid to our firm was large enough to ensure that we complied with the instructions. We hope that this makes more sense to you than it does to us."

Tucker picked up the yellowed envelope, addressed to him at the Gonzales lab. Carefully, he peeled up the flap, an easy task since the glue had dried out during the years. He pulled the single page from the envelope and read it.

"Tuck," it began, "we have been trapped in the past, in 1836, by Isaac Millsaps and a number of his corporate cronies. Their idea was to win the Battle of the Alamo for H. Perot Lewis. A man named Brown and his mercenaries kept that from happening, but they decided to remain in the past to prevent Lewis from using the transference system for his own reasons again.

"All of us, that is Mary Jo, Bob and I, have decided that it won't hurt for us to return to the future. We used this method to contact you so that the mercenaries won't know what we have done.

"The best date would probably be at the close of the Texas War for Independence. We have decided to be at the chapel of the Alamo on May 2, 1836. Please come and get us. This whole thing wasn't our fault."

The letter was signed, "Andy Kent."

Tucker set his cigar in the ashtray and let it burn. He stared at the letter from his assistants and felt sick to his stomach. There was no way that he could go to 1836. His Integrated Trans-Spacio-Temporal Physical Transference System could send people into the past, and it could retrieve them, but when it brought them back, it killed them. That was the reason that Tucker had been out of the lab when the equipment was used by the corporation. The Corporation didn't want him there to stop the transference when they used it to send their mercenaries into the past to fight the Battle of the Alamo.

That left Tucker with a problem. Did he send a message to the past to Andy Kent, Mary Jo Andross and Bob Cunningham to tell them about the problems of retrieval, or did he just leave them there, thinking he would come for them sometime? Did he answer their plea right away, or search for an answer to the problem first. After all, he reasoned, he had all the time in the world.

TWO

The morning of May 2, 1836 dawned with scattered clouds on the horizon. Andy Kent, a tall, slender man with close-cut hair, and a small moustache, stood with the reins of his horse held in his left hand. Kent had bright blue eyes, a narrow face and a slightly pointed chin. He turned and looked up at his two friends, then put a hand to his eyes to shade them from the sun. He wore a shirt of undyed cotton, dark wool pants, leather boots, and a small straw hat.

"Going to be a hot one," said Bob Cunningham. Cunningham was a smaller, stockier man. He had let his beard, once neatly trimmed, get away from him so that it covered the lower half of his face in a mass of brown, flowing curls. He was seated on his horse, binoculars to his dark eyes as he stared down at the ruined mission. He was wearing clothing similar to Kent's, had topped it off with a tan hat that looked stolen from Indiana Jones.

Mary Jo Andross didn't speak. She was a slender brun-

5

ette who bordered on skinny. She had lost weight since
their transference into 1836. Her long, dark hair hung
nearly to her waist. Like Kent, she had a narrow face, a
pointed chin and a tiny nose. She was dressed like the two
men. A rough cotton shirt that was tan, pants that had been
rolled up twice, boots and a hat. After watching the slaugh-
ter of humans in the butcher yard that had been the chapel
courtyard of the Alamo, she had become quieter, almost
brooding.

"What'd you think?" asked Kent. "Just ride on down
there?"

Cunningham lowered his binoculars and tucked them
into a soft, fur case. He took off his hat and pulled a
checkered cloth from his pocket and wiped the sweat from
the headband.

"Seems to be deserted now. Caught a little movement in
the town, but nothing around the fort."

"Mary Jo?"

"What?"

"You up to this?"

She shrugged. "What's to be up to? We agreed on the
location because it was one that we could find easily and so
could Tuck. Let's just do it."

Kent swung himself up into his saddle, and dug his
heels into the flanks of his horse. He pulled on the reins,
turned the horse to the left, and began the gentle descent
toward the Alamo.

The old fort, a Spanish mission actually, was spread
over three acres. Various soldiers, in an attempt to turn it
into a fort, had constructed firing platforms, closed the perimeter with log barricades, erected cannon emplacements,
and fortified some of the eight-foot-high walls. The
chapel's walls were twelve feet high, and that one structure
dominated most of the courtyard.

They rode down, along the west wall, where there had been a large tree, now gone, and turned back to the east. They came to the gate which hung open, the wood shattered in the final assault on the fort.

They stopped outside for a moment. Kent looked at the thick adobe walls of the mission, pockmarked and scarred by rifle, musket and cannon fire. There were rust-colored stains along part of it, some looking like water splashed from the top, or thrown against the adobe. He didn't say anything to Andross. He recognized the stains as dried blood. A lot of people had done a lot of bleeding to create those markings.

Kent slipped from his saddle, stepped over the remains of a small earthen barricade that had been built outside the gate, and looked through to the interior. He saw nothing, and went in. The ground under his feet was soft and beginning to turn green. He reached out and touched the rough wall. He glanced over his shoulder, saw both Cunningham and Andross sitting on their horses, and then continued until he was standing in the courtyard.

He hadn't thought it would affect him. He thought he was beyond the emotions that suddenly threatened to overwhelm him. He let his eyes roam, seeing everything and noticing almost nothing. There was evidence of fire in some of the rooms around the walls. Cannonball damage everywhere. A breach in the north wall that had threatened to let the entire Mexican Army through. Holes in walls. Hundreds of pockmarks where shot had bounced off. Ragged stains on the walls, and clumps of weeds that showed where men had fallen and bled.

Kent felt something in his throat, felt a cold hand on his stomach and wasn't sure whether he was going to be able to maintain his composure. As a kid he had walked the Custer Battlefield, but this was different. It was a fight that he had taken part in. A fight where he had watched the men die. In that moment, he understood completely just what Andross had to feel.

The voice behind him startled him. He spun, and saw Cunningham standing in the arch of the gate. "What's happening?"

"You see anything?" asked Cunningham.

Kent shook his head. "No. It's deserted. Nobody here except the ghosts." He hesitated, and then said it again. "Just the ghosts."

"I'll get Mary Jo."

"Bob, wait," said Kent.

"Wait for what?"

"Look around," he said. "Don't you feel anything?"

"Andy, what's to feel? We've got to get in to wait for Tuck. Is there a problem with that?"

Kent didn't answer right away. He watched his friend and then looked back toward the chapel. "No, I guess there isn't," he said. "Maybe one of us should take Mary Jo into town and find her something to eat. All three of us don't have to be here."

"Yes we do," said Cunningham. "Besides, we can't protect her forever. She'll have to deal with this and it might be best, for her, if she is standing right there when Tuck pops in and says, 'Hey, let's go home.'"

Kent took a deep breath and exhaled noisily. "Maybe you're right. Let's just get it done."

They tethered their horses near the cannon emplacement that had guarded the south gate. Now there were grasses and weeds growing there, giving the horses something to eat. Together the three of them walked across the open courtyard, through the gate of a short wall that separated the main part of the Alamo from the chapel and then sat in the shade to wait. When they had written the letter, it never occurred to them to specify a time for the meeting. Kent had just assumed that it would be about noon.

Kent picked up a handful of pebbles and began chucking them at the chapel walls. Most of them bounced in the dirt, kicking up tiny clouds of dust that were swept away by a light breeze. Without meaning to, he was studying the chapel's facade. It was as pockmarked as the rest of the fort. The top had been torn away by the cannonade, and the front doors, thick wooden things that had been shattered in the final attack, hung open. Through them he could see that more of the roof had collapsed and rubble choked the interior.

And just like the rest of the old fort, there were rust-colored stains smeared on the adobe. Bloodstains. So many of them. It was decidedly strange sitting there, watching the clouds building and blowing over the top of the chapel, looking at the evidence of the recent battle.

Finally, Cunningham reached out and stopped Kent. "Let's just forget about the rocks for a while. Okay?"

Kent looked at him and said, "Oh. Sorry." He glanced at Andross who had dropped to the ground, almost as if unconscious. She sat with her legs spread, her hands by her sides, and her eyes focused on the ground between her knees.

It was infecting them all. The ghosts of the Alamo were getting to each of them. And then, near the ruined doors of the battered chapel, there was a bright shimmering like desert heat rising from sunbaked pavement. It took on a vaguely human shape, seemed to solidify, vanish and then came back. Finally, standing there, holding a single sheet of fragile paper was a woman.

"That's not Tuck," said Cunningham.

Kent climbed to his feet, took a step back so that he was leaning against the wall. "No, it's not," he said, as if answering a question.

"Then who the hell is it?"

"I don't know," said Kent. "But she's obviously using the Tucker Transfer, so she's one of us."

The eerie, yellowish glow that had engulfed the woman dissipated slowly and when it was gone, she stepped forward smiling. She wore a form-fitting, emerald green jumpsuit that didn't exactly mold itself to her shape, but seemed to bend and shift with her movements. One moment it was stretched tightly over her and the next loosely draped from her shoulders and hips.

She was a tall woman, almost six feet, had shoulder-length brown hair and dark, brown eyes. Her face was angular and her nose almost too small for her face.

She held out the paper as if it was a talisman and said in English that had a strange accent, "You posted this? Sent it?"

Cunningham was the first to react. He was unsure of what to do, so he stood his ground and said, "We are responsible for it, yes." He assumed that it was the letter that they had sent to Tucker. What else could it be.

"Then we have work to do," she informed them.

"Where's Doctor Tucker?" asked Andross, her voice unnaturally high and strained. "Why didn't he come with you?"

"I guess the easiest thing is to tell you that Doctor Tucker was unavailable for this journey." She held out the letter, letting it flap gently in the breeze. "He provided this so that you would know that we are his, ah, representatives."

"What do you mean unavailable?" asked Cunningham. "Is he sick? What?"

"Just that he couldn't make this journey. All your questions will be answered in time."

Kent took the letter from her fingers. The ink was faded, hard to read in the bright sunlight, but he recognized it. There was no question about it. It was the letter they had sent to Tucker so that he would rescue them.

"I guess there is no reason not to believe you," said Kent, slowly. He studied the woman again, his eyes meeting hers and he thought that he had never seen eyes so brown and lovely. As he handed the letter back, he said, "Let's just get out of here."

"Well," she said, avoiding his eyes, "it's not quite that easy. There are a few things that you have to know."

"Such as?" asked Cunningham, suspicious.

The woman looked around, as if searching for something. "Not a comfortable place for us to talk, is it?"

"We weren't expecting to talk," said Kent harshly. Then he realized that he shouldn't have snapped at her. "We were expecting a retrieval. We thought that someone would appear first, to check out the situation, but we didn't expect a long discussion about it. And that still doesn't tell us where Tuck is, or who the hell you are."

She ignored the questions again and said, "Before we can initiate your final retrieval, there are a couple of things that have to be done . . ."

"No," snapped Andross. "We will do nothing else in the past. We've done too much already. We don't have the right to make changes because we don't understand all the possibilities, all the ramifications that goes with it."

The woman smiled. "No," she agreed, "we don't have

the right, but we do have the responsibility to put things back the way they should be."

"You mean you want us to fight the Battle of the Alamo again?" asked Kent.

"No, not the Alamo," she said. "Gettysburg."

THREE

Robert Kevin Brown sat in the parlor of a Philadelphia house and listened to the sound of the traffic moving outside. Metal-shod horses' hooves and wooden wheels with metal rims against cobblestones. The window of the parlor was open, a gentle breeze blowing in but failing to cool the interior. There were no screens on the windows, and the insects were blowing in too.

Brown, a big man with blond hair and gray eyes, sat on the stiff-backed couch and brushed at a fly that hovered around his head. He folded the newspaper over, amazed at the journalistic style of the day which allowed, nearly demanded, that the reporter contribute his own thoughts and ideas.

There was another call for the United States to intervene in the unstable situation in Texas. Brown smiled at that, knowing that it would be ten years before the U.S. would fight Mexico over the issue of Texas.

13

There was a quiet tapping on the hardwood floor outside the parlor and Brown looked up to see Jessie Thompson. She was one of the mercenaries sent into the past with him to fight the Mexicans at the Alamo. A tall woman, maybe five-seven or eight, light hair that was now down to the middle of her back, she was wearing a brown dress. She had bright blue eyes, a long nose and full lips. Her face was round and framed by her hair.

She moved into the parlor, a room that was sparsely furnished, and with rows of books along one wall. New books that were considered classics in her day, but now considered the lowest form of entertainment. Polite people went to the theatre, sometimes read the newspaper, but stayed away from novels. She consoled herself by telling herself that *Moby Dick* wouldn't be written for more than a decade.

Brown held the paper out and said, "More debate about the Texas issue. Still writing about the Alamo and what should be done about it."

Thompson sat down in one of the two wing-back chairs, adjusted her skirts and petticoats and then frowned. "This is a fine period. *Your* major problem is fighting the buttons on your pants, but I have to wear nineteen layers of everything, bind myself into corsets and work like hell to keep you from seeing my ankles," she said, picking up the strings of their earlier discussion.

Brown folded the paper and set it on the rounded table next to him. A small thing of dark browns and clawed feet. There was a white doily in the center of it and a kerosene lamp on it. He stood up and moved toward the bookcases. He touched a couple of the volumes, wishing for a good Poe story, or an H.G. Wells, or Jules Verne, but it was too early for any of those.

"Sometimes I think we made a mistake," said Brown. "Maybe we should have gone home. This is . . ."

"It's too late to worry about that now," said Thompson. "We decided together that we would stay in 1836 to deny Lewis the knowledge that he was successful."

Brown wiped the sweat from his forehead and wished that he had central air, a refrigerator full of cold beer, an electric fan, anything.

"But it's not too late," said Brown. "I've been thinking about this for a long time. There are a couple of ways for us to get home, if we want to."

Thompson shook her head. "No. We have to stay. If even one of us goes back, then Lewis knows and we make him the most powerful man the world has ever known."

"Sometimes I think that is a load of crap," said Brown. "We go back, we don't have to talk to Lewis. We don't have to see him, and if we do, we lie. Tell him there was nothing we could do. History can't be changed."

"Even though we know that it can," said Thompson.

Brown moved from the books and sat behind the oak desk. It had a large central drawer flanked by two smaller doors on either side. There were thin, curved legs. On the desk was a green blotter stained with ink, a couple of quills and a bottle of ink. A lamp stood on it and the ceiling over it was smeared with the soot from it. He touched the calendar for 1836 and wondered when the investments would begin to pay off. He wondered why he even gave a fuck because he knew what was going to happen. He'd read all about it in the history books.

He fingered one of the quills idly, watching it. "Lewis shouldn't even know that he sent us. Any change we introduce will affect him just as it does everyone else. He won't know it."

"Bob, you're guessing. We don't have any idea what the

ramifications would be. The safest course is for us to stay in this time and make the best of it."

"Come on, Jessie, you were just complaining about the feminine clothing. Wouldn't you like to be able to wear shorts in the summer? A bikini or a mini-skirt? Wouldn't you like to go to a movie, ride in a car? Hell, wouldn't you like to just sit in the living room and watch something mindless on TV?"

Now she smiled. "Or eat ice cream. Or use the microwave. Or fly to the Bahamas. Or get a job without everyone thinking that I'm demented. Hell, yes, I would like all those things. But we agreed. All of us agreed."

Brown rocked back in the chair and laced his fingers behind his head. "You know what I miss the most? Really miss. I think it's M and Ms. Isn't that ridiculous. We're living in a primitive world and I miss chocolate candy."

"I think I miss zippers the most. It takes twenty minutes to button and snap everything."

"And ballpoint pens," said Brown. "In the movies, they always managed to write volumes without getting ink on their hands. I try to sign my name and it looks like I've bathed in the stuff."

"Or MTV," said Thompson getting caught up in the spirit of the moment. "Would you believe that I used to watch MTV?"

"Flush toilets. Just a splash of water and the whole thing is gone."

"A toaster," said Thompson. "I hate to have toast burned and I haven't figured out how to toast it in that wood-burning monstrosity in the kitchen."

"I could give you a list of a hundred things. A thousand. I sat in here one night, the foul odor from the city blowing in the window along with the bugs, and made a list. A long list." He saw the look on her face and held up a hand.

"Don't worry. I burned it before I went up to bed. Couldn't have someone asking me to explain all-night movies, radio, jets, TV dinners, and the like."

"I know what you're doing," said Thompson. "You're trying to make me homesick. Well, it won't work."

Brown was going to challenge her on that point. He was going to prove that he could make her homesick, but the bell on the front door jangled. He pushed himself out of his chair and said, "That'll be the postman with the morning delivery. Now maybe I'll find out how much money we've made in the last few weeks."

Thompson caught him by the parlor door. She put a hand on his sleeve and said, "It's not that easy for me. Not that easy at all."

"I know," he responded. "But I think that if we work our way through it carefully, we could go home with Lewis none the wiser. It's just something to think about."

She nodded. "Yes, it is. And it's almost all that I've been thinking about for the last several weeks."

FOUR

"Now just a damned minute," said Kent.

"No," said the woman. "You must listen to everything before you make up your mind. We don't want you to change the outcome of the battle. No, that's not true. What we want is for you to put it back the way it was. Make the Union win."

Cunningham hopped up so that he was sitting on the short wall that separated the chapel courtyard from the rest of the Alamo. The sunlight, periodically blotted out by the high, fast-moving clouds, created interesting patterns in the dirt and on the chapel. He watched the dancing displays for a moment and then asked, "Why don't we discuss this at the lab? You can lay the whole thing out for us there."

"Power requirements," said the woman. "Besides, you have to find the mercenaries and organize them so that they can be of help to the Union. Hit the key points like Little

Round Top, Pickett's Charge and Custer's fight at Hanover."

Kent, who was standing with his arms folded, shook his head. He studied her carefully, watching the way the sun highlighted the blond streaks in her brown hair, shook his head. "We're not doing a thing until we've talked to Tuck."

The woman ignored that and asked, "Do any of you know anything about the battle?"

"I know that it was fought during the beginning of July in 1863," said Cunningham. "I know the Union won, or is considered to have won because Lee withdrew from the field, and I know that the main reason the Union won was because they made the fewest mistakes."

"Don't let her draw you into a conversation about this, Bob," said Kent.

But she answered Cunningham. "Now, it is the Union who blundered the most and lost as Pickett drove through the center of their line while Rebel sharpshooters poured a devastating rifle fire into the Union position from both Round Tops. With that defeat, the Union slid into a collapse that ended with Doubleday's surrender at Albany in 1866."

"Doubleday? Albany? The only Doubleday I know invented baseball, although I think there was a general by that name in the Civil War."

Kent forgot what he had told Cunningham and jumped in. "And I remember the Civil War ending in April of 1865 in Virginia."

"So you see the problem," said the woman. "I will forward a briefing package to you. It'll explain all the ramifications of a Southern victory. I might say that it is much more widespread than just a Rebel victory in the Civil War."

With that she moved to the rear, to the spot where she had appeared, almost like an actor searching for her mark on the stage.

"Wait," called Cunningham. "We haven't agreed to anything. We want to speak to Tuck."

Kent took a step forward and called, "Who are you? You didn't tell us your name."

The woman held up her hand as if to wave, her eyes locked on Kent. As she smiled, she was again encased in a golden glow that appeared at the top of her head and spread slowly to her feet. For a moment she seemed to be held static, looking like a poorly developed photograph of herself, and then, with an audible pop, she vanished, taking nearly a cubic yard of Alamo dirt with her. A shallow crater three feet across remained, smoking slightly.

An instant later, the glow returned. In its sphere was a single object that appeared at what had been ground level. It dropped into the crater.

Cunningham hopped off the wall and walked to the crater. Laying in the bottom of it was a book with an envelope stuck in it. Cunningham reached for it and turned it over. The title said, *The History of the United States 1860–2000.*

FIVE

Steven Dennison sat in his room at the boarding house in Atlanta, Georgia, and continued to write. He ventured out only to eat and to buy more paper and ink. The rest of the day he sat at a table he used as a desk, scratching at the paper with his quill pens. He got up at dawn because he found the flickering light from the candles to be too annoying for him to work.

He glanced over his shoulder, as the sounds of the city drifted up to him. Children yelling as they chased a yapping dog down the street. A man calling out the latest headlines from the newspaper. Horses and carts traveling. The rhythmic booming of a drum as someone beat it for some unknown reason.

Dennison walked to the window and looked out on the street. He could see the front yard of the rooming house, a flagstone walk from a white picket fence to the porch, a pathway along the dirt street.

The one thing that always amazed him was the noise. He had thought of the past as a quiet, peaceful time, when the people moved slowly, reasoning out their actions carefully. But the pace wasn't that much slower. Here, they only had the hours of daylight to accomplish their tasks, and they rushed to finish before the sun set. Oh, there were candles and lamps, but they just didn't give the light needed to see, and it was easier to start business at sunrise and conclude it by sundown.

And without all the modern conveniences, people had to work harder to accomplish less than a lazy man in the future could do in an hour.

He wanted to jerk down the window to cut off the noise, but didn't dare. It was hot enough in the room already and if he shut out the little breeze there was, it would be like a sauna in less than an hour.

He moved back to his desk and took off the rough cotton shirt, hanging it on the back of the wooden chair. As he sat down, the chair creaked, sounding like it was on the verge of collapse. He turned back to his work, a complete history of the War Between the States. Or at least as complete as he could make it, working from his memory. In twenty-five years, it would be 1861 and the South would begin the war. Dennison wanted to be ready. He smiled at the paper, thinking of the battlecry that had rung through his high school, and even his college. It had been a joke then, but it was no longer. The South *would* rise again.

Lemuel Crawford leaned against the handle of his shovel and looked at the four other, sweating men in front of him. He turned to stare at the line of the ditch they had dug that morning, the moist brown dirt piled by the trench and the puddles where the water was seeping in. He pulled the rag from his hip pocket, wiped his hands and then examined the blisters on them.

"Christ," he said. He mopped his face and then bent back to work. It wasn't quite noon, and his shoulders ached, his arms hurt, his hands stung, and he felt like he was going to pass out. He looked longingly at the water bucket with its tin dipper and knew that he couldn't stop for another drink already. The foreman had warned him about it the last time, threatening to fire him for laziness. But there was cotton in his mouth from thirst, and he could feel the sun sapping his strength.

He tossed a shovelful of dirt out of the trench and then swore under his breath. "Four fucking years in college and the only thing I can find to do is digging ditches."

Of course, it wasn't that his four years of college were worthless. It was the damned poker game. Crawford still fumed about being taken like a rube fresh from the hills. He had been sucked into the game figuring that these hicks wouldn't have any idea about what they were doing. He had watched as they systematically took all his gold, his pocket watch, and tried to get his pistol. A Browning P-35 that held fourteen rounds and was decidedly out of place.

"Damn!" he growled, again angry with himself. He felt his stomach flutter and he wanted to smash something, anything. "Stupid. Stupid. Stupid."

"You say something," asked one of the other men. He was stripped to the waist and sweating heavily. His arms looked as big as most men's thighs. He flipped the shovel, even when loaded with dirt, like it weighed nothing.

"Just talking to myself," said Crawford.

"You two want to stop gabbing and get back to work? You don't want this job, I can find a couple of other men who would be happy to have the work."

Crawford didn't respond and didn't look up. He just

kept working his shovel, throwing the dirt a little harder than before as if to prove that he wasn't tired and that he really wanted the job.

"Damn," he said again.

William Summers sat in the restaurant of the Baltimore Hotel and looked at the eggs, pancakes, steak and ham in front of him. Sitting across from him was Meg Clark who was sipping at her tea.

Summers put down his fork and said, "It would seem to me that you'd appreciate not having to work."

"Well, you fit right into this time," she said. "You *would* think that it's just marvelous to sit in all those fancy offices watching all you men smoke lousy cigars and make big deals. I just sit and nod and pretend that I don't know a thing."

He studied her across the table. A petite blonde with her long hair piled high on her head. Her green eyes burned out at him. That, combined with her light complexion, up-turned nose and rounded face made her a good-looking woman. He tried to overlook the fact that she could probably take him in a fair fight. Her scores on the unarmed combat portion of their training had been that much better than his.

She waited for him to say something, and when he didn't speak, she said, "This is a lousy time to be living. Nothing is happening. The big event of the period was the battle we fought. Now we're supposed to earn big money because we know what's going to happen, but everyone seems to forget that a major depression begins next year."

Summers set his fork down and picked up his napkin. He patted his lips and said, "What do you want to do about it?"

"I don't know." She shook her head. "But this isn't

what I expected when we agreed to remain here. I mean we all made jokes about going to California and buying a mill. Or investing in the railroads. Except that there won't be a gold rush in California for another, ah, thirteen years. Railroads won't come into their own for a decade. Morse won't invent the telegraph for eight years."

"The point, Meg," said Summers.

"The point is, there is nothing for us to do. We can't make our big investments and get rich for another ten years, or twenty years. And, if something happens to you, I'm expected to sit around the house in mourning for the rest of my life. I can't go to work. I can't handle the investments. I would have to find a man to do that for me."

"The point, for Christ's sake."

"Let's go back. Back to the future where we belong. I feel so out of place here. They won't let me do a thing. Hell, there's even a law against women smoking in public."

"You don't smoke,"

"And couldn't even if I wanted to. They don't allow it."

Summers held up a hand to stop her and said, "Just for the minute let's suppose that we decide you're right. It's not like we can go down to the station and hop on the next bus leaving for the future."

Clark sat forward and leaned across the table. She put a hand up as if to flag Summer's attention. "But we can do the next best thing. We know where the beacon is. We just go back to Texas and get it. Activate it and the next thing we know, we're home."

"What about the others?" asked Summers.

"What do you mean?"

"What if some of them want to go back. If we use the beacon, they're stuck here, in 1836."

"No," said Clark. "Once we're in the future, we can return the beacon in case someone else wants to use it."

Summers picked up his fork and finished his breakfast. The eggs were rubbery, the steak was tough and over-cooked, the ham salted almost into non-existence, and the coffee tasted like mud. The total price for the meal, including the cigar, would come to nearly seventy-five cents.

While he ate, he thought about what Meg had said. He realized that he wasn't really happy in 1836. She had been right. The time was dull. They were about ten years early for the industrial revolution and the coming boom. In fact, if he had to pick a time to live, this one would be at the bottom of the list.

"Even if you don't want to go with me," said Clark, "I think I'll take off anyway."

"Let's think this through first," said Summers. Like most of them, he hadn't been convinced that remaining in the past was the best idea. The thought had been pushed by Brown and Thompson and it seemed to be something they wanted. He didn't understand the reason, but he had gone along with it at the time.

Clark stood up and faced him. "Look, if you're really happy here, then stay. I just can't take it anymore."

Summers followed suit and dug into his pocket for a silver dollar. He dropped it on the table and then looked at it. In his own time that could easily be worth ten or twenty thousand dollars. He had a pocketful of change that might bring a hundred thousand dollars at home.

That was a tempting thought. Grab a handful of change so that he would be rich in his own era, but that wasn't the deciding factor. It was remembering a scene in the long barracks of the Alamo. Brown sitting on a table. Thompson wandering around near him, explaining why they all had to stay in 1836. A long drawn-out meeting in the dusty room with the sunlight fading. A meeting where they all agreed that they should remain in 1836 because clever people could make a lot of money. They knew what was going to happen for the next hundred and fifty years.

Except no one had thought to say that nothing would happen for ten years. It just wasn't what he expected. So he tossed a buck on the table and followed Clark out of the restaurant, passed a couple of men in dark clothing with full beards and long hair, standing in the lobby of the hotel, watching Clark walk across the floor.

He caught her near the front door. The doorman, a huge person in a bright blue coat opened the door and waited. The sound from the street, the voices, the horses hooves, the shouting, blew in the door.

"Meg," he said, "I'm with you. Let's blow this pop stand and see about getting home."

"You mean it?"

"Sure. Why wouldn't I?"

She grabbed his arm, thought about the people in the lobby who weren't used to seeing others touching in public. Thought about the people who were convinced that affection should only be displayed in the home, and let go.

"When?"

Now Summers smiled. "Let me change some of our gold for the local coin of the realm, and dig up our weapons. I figure we can leave this afternoon."

"Great!"

SIX

Cunningham reached down and picked the book out of the crater. He had expected it to be hot, for no good reason. Maybe it was the golden glow that suggested heat, or maybe it was the smoking of the crater. It made no difference because the book was only sun-warm.

He flipped through it, glancing at items from the Civil War through the Second World War. As he read through it, he felt himself grow sick. He rocked back, on his heels and then sat down, dizzy. History as he knew it was badly flawed. The big break with real history came in the middle of the Civil War and from there it expanded outward with increasing intensity until the world of 1950 was so topsy turvy that he failed to recognize it.

"Bob, what is it?" asked Kent. "You okay?"

"It's this," said Cunningham, holding the book up like it was a banner. "It's this."

Kent crouched next to him and took the book from his

hands. He flipped it open to a page detailing a battle of the Second World War and realized that he had never heard of it. A battle that took place in Spain with British and French soldiers fighting Germans. The Spaniards were on both sides. There were airplanes involved. Suddenly, he knew exactly how Cunningham felt.

"Guys," said Andross. "What is it?"

Cunningham took the book back and opened it to the front page, looking at the table of contents, and then thumbing through it.

"Bob? What's wrong?"

"Better sit down, Mary Jo. It's not good news."

"What is it?" she asked again.

"We've really fucked it up. I don't know what we did, but we've really fucked it up, starting, apparently, at Gettysburg. Somehow the Rebels win there, and from that point it all goes to hell."

"And then?" asked Andross.

"And then," repeated Cunningham, flipping through the book, "the South wins the war in 1866 just as the woman said. Lincoln wasn't assassinated because the country was split in two, just as he feared it would be. You want a shock, come and take a look at this map of the United States."

Andross knelt behind Cunningham, looking over his shoulder. The map showed the U.S. almost intact from the Mason-Dixon Line north and to the Mississippi River. Missouri was divided, a concession to the South after the war. Everything from Montana south through Wyoming, Colorado and New Mexico didn't exist. Both Canada and Mexico had taken advantage of the loss of the Civil War, expanding their borders. On the west coast, California, along with part of Nevada and Arizona, existed as part of the United States, but Oregon and Washington were gone.

"What—" she said.

"Listen," said Cunningham. "After the Civil War the newly established Confederate States of America, recognized within weeks by Germany, Spain, France, and Russia, guaranteed a number of homelands for the Indian Tribes that assisted them." He smiled, "That explains the hole in the middle of the country."

He flipped through the book again, stopping and pointing a number of times. "Look, there was no Spanish-American War. The First World War lasted until 1921. The Communists, who took over Russia in 1917, came in on the side of the Allies to help defeat the Germans. That gave rise to Hitler and the Second World War, but there was no United States like there was supposed to be. We're just a fragmented entity that didn't have the industrial might, so Hitler wasn't defeated . . ."

"Good God!" said Andross.

"You don't know the half of it," said Cunningham. "You remember the division between the North and the South after the Civil War, all the troubles between the two areas of one country? Imagine what it must have been like for two separate countries. We're talking borders and passports and two standing armies with defense treaties with other countries in the world. By 1950, the whole complexion of the planet had changed. Hitler wasn't beaten in 1945. No atomic bombs dropped on Japan, but three were dropped. One on L.A., one on Dayton, and one on London."

"Jesus," said Kent.

"And all of it seems to trace back to Gettysburg. That seems to be where the critical change was introduced," said Cunningham. "As near as I can tell, everything from 1860 to that point is just as it's supposed to be. I don't remember that much about the Civil War before Gettysburg, but it

doesn't seem that anything there has been changed. The
Rebels won at Bull Run just as they were supposed to. I
wish I had a way of cross-checking it, but I can't."

"So what do we do?" asked Kent.

"The woman said that something happened in 1863 that
changed the outcome of the war and radically altered history and it seems that she knows what she's talking about.
All she wants us to do is put things back the way they
belong."

"Bob," said Andross, "let's just get out of here for now.
We can figure all this out later."

"In a minute," said Cunningham. "In a minute. We've
got to think about this. Decide what we're going to do."

"Isn't it obvious?" asked Kent. "We have to do what she
asked us to do. Make a change to fix the future. I mean,
put it back the way it's supposed to be. She's not asking us
to change it, but to fix it."

Kent got to his feet, feeling the urge to walk, to pace.
He stepped to the chapel door and peered inside. There
were piles of broken adobe lying around. There were
splintered beams sprouting at odd angles. And there was
the ramp built by Green Jameson and his engineers for a
cannon emplacement overlooking the wall. He turned and
walked toward the remains of the log palisade that Davy
Crockett had guarded and looked at the open fields rising
gently to the south. The Mexican Army had formed there
to begin their assault.

He thought about that, about the men he had known.
The defenders of the Alamo. William Travis, Jim Bowie,
James Butler Bonham, and all the rest. He thought about
time travel and changes in the past. About seemingly insig-
nificant acts that rippled and echoed through the years until
the future bore no resemblance to anything he remembered.

He turned and walked back to the crater where Cunningham sat with the book in his lap as if afraid to read anymore of it. "How in the hell did this happen?" he asked.

Cunningham shrugged. "How in the hell would I know?"

"But the changes don't factor in until after 1863," said Kent.

"You notice that 1863 is really 1836 with the last two numbers reversed," said Andross.

"You suggesting that means something, Mary Jo?" asked Cunningham.

"No, I guess not. Can't see how that would affect time," she said. "Just an interesting point."

"You know we have to make the change," said Cunningham. There is no way around it." He got to his feet and brandished the book. "Besides, this says that any changes we make could only put history back on the right path. We sure as hell couldn't fuck it up anymore than it already is."

Kent shook his head. He hadn't been listening. "It's that damned letter. She had it, but she didn't say a thing about Tuck. She just kept waving it like it was magic."

"I can't see where that makes any difference," said Cunningham. "We have to make the change and if they transport us to 1863, we're that much closer to home."

"Then you're suggesting we do what she wants?" asked Andross, surprised that Cunningham would advocate any change in time.

"Of course. We have to," he said. "And anyway, all we're asked to do right now is round up the team."

"A fairly difficult task," said Kent, "with no telephones or telegraph or national postal system or fast, convenient ways to travel. Shit, how are we supposed to find any of those people?"

Cunningham shrugged and turned toward the main courtyard of the Alamo, where the horses were tethered. "That man, Brown, the leader, said that he was going to Philadelphia. That would seem to be the place to start."'

"Wait," said Kent.

Cunningham stopped walking and looked back. "What's to wait?"

"Why do we have to travel through 1836 America to carry out this plan? Why don't they just take us home, fly us to Philadelphia and then return us to 1836. Hell, with a good computer research facility we could probably pin-point the majority of the people in an hour. For that matter, why the fuck do we need to do it? They know what the problem is. Let them fix it."

"Hell, Andy, I don't have the answers. Maybe they need someone trained in this sort of work. How many groups of mercenaries who have time-traveled can there be? Maybe we did such a good job blending in that they want to use us again."

"None of that makes sense," said Kent. "I can think of a dozen questions that need to be answered. A hundred."

Cunningham set the book on the wall and leaned back, folding his arms. "This isn't the place to get into a debate about the paradoxes of time travel. Or ask questions about the woman or Tuck. For your dozen questions, there might easily be a dozen good answers, if we had them. All I'm saying is let's see if we can put the team back together and go from there. We haven't committed to doing anything."

"Mary Jo?" said Kent. "What do you think?" He could see that she still wasn't feeling well and didn't know if it was being in the Alamo a second time or if it was seeing the fucked up future that was supposed to be their home.

"Bob's right," she said. "We haven't committed ourselves to a thing, but if we don't act now, there won't be a chance for us. We can assemble the mercenaries and when we get more information, decide what we want to do."

"Then I guess I'm outvoted," said Kent. He moved close to the wall and touched the book again. "I suppose we have to try to do something if we're able. We can't leave history the way it is now. It's not right."

SEVEN

The woman, still wearing her bright green jumpsuit, sat in the tiny office that was bathed in the glow of fluorescence, sipping at the tepid coffee. She waited while her boss, David Jackson, a tall, skinny man with huge hands and no sense of humor, dug through a pile of computer printouts. When he found what he wanted, he turned, set the printout on the small desk, picked up his own coffee and then waited.

The woman felt the silence grow, spreading like a cancer and knew she had to say something just to be saying something. "They weren't very receptive."

"What'd you expect, Maddie? They thought that this Tucker person was going to be along to rescue them. If not him, then someone they recognized."

"But they saw the letter," she protested. "The one they sent Tucker."

Jackson rocked back in his chair and turned toward the

wall where the window would have been if they had been above ground, and could have gotten clearances for it from the Environmental Safety Commission, the Commission on the Study of Hazardous Panoramas on Sentient Thought, and the Governor's Board.

"You handled that poorly. You—"

"That's not fair," she snapped. "I was sent in with explicit instructions. I couldn't lie to them, but I had to deceive them. They are intelligent people. They saw through me. Especially that Andy Kent."

Jackson turned and typed a command into the computer. A moment later the information he was seeking was parading across the screen in neat rows of numbers. When he found the sequence he wanted, he hit the escape key and then pointed at the screen.

"Even with the book, which was an additional risk to transmit, but even with the book, the odds are that they will do nothing."

Maddie stood and stepped to the left so that she was standing next to a metal rack loaded with history books, theoretical studies on historical possibilities, and a half dozen volumes that were obtained through time travel. The latter had bright red covers that contained microchips that would cause them to disintegrate it someone tried to remove them from the office.

With the piles of computer printouts, the desk and chair, and the small, tubular steel chair for visitors, every square inch of floor space was covered. Maddie glanced at her feet and saw that she was standing on two copies of the same book. One written before the change was introduced at Gettysburg and the second written after. It was how they had pinpointed the problem.

Maddie slumped back into the chair and picked up the

books, setting them on her lap. She flipped open one and began reading it, ignoring Jackson.

"You never explained to me how you got both books," she said. "I don't understand it."

"What's not to understand," said Jackson, his tone soothing, like talking to someone he wanted to remain calm.

"If a change is introduced in 1863, all the books written after that point should reflect the change. Therefore, any change that we read about, we wouldn't have been aware of because it would have been made before any of us were born."

"Yes, that is correct. If there was someone messing around in the past, we would have no way of knowing it. And if we traveled to 1863 to watch, then we would see the history happening just as we expected it to happen because the change would be introduced then and we wouldn't know. And if we traveled back and stopped in, say 1990, to buy a history book, it would reflect that change."

"Exactly," said Maddie, running a hand through her hair. She didn't like talking about the theories of time travel because of all the paradoxes. She usually felt that she was arguing in circles, which was exactly what she was doing.

"Now suppose that I'm a scientist, and I've run a computer check on the course of history. The computer, for some reason, isn't happy with the outcome of a specific event. It says, for some reason, that such and such should not have logically followed such and such. In other words, history has taken a decidedly bizarre path."

"Like what?"

Jackson got to his feet, put his hands behind his back like he was about to lecture a college class. "Take a battle. One side has the position, a vastly superior force, better supply lines and better lines of communications. Everything on their side, but they lose. The computer flags that."

"So they lost because their leadership was worse, or they weren't fighting for a cause they believed in, or God wasn't with them. The other side had these things working for it," said Maddie.

"Of course, and history is littered with such events, but to the computer, they don't make sense, so the computer flags them. Then I check them out."

Maddie shook her head. "Doesn't matter. You go back in time, you're going back to the past that you already know because the change has already been introduced."

"That's right," said Jackson grinning, as if he was about to spring a trap.

"So your research doesn't give you two copies of the same history book with widely different views."

"Except one was bought after the invention of time travel and the other before."

"You've lost me because both were written after the change."

"Yes, but if I travel to the 1950 United States and hop off my machine, I've arrived in a time before it was possible for the change to have taken place because the instrument of the change, the Tucker Transfer, hasn't been invented yet. I'm in a virgin time, so to speak."

"But that is still after 1863," insisted Maddie.

"Of course it is, and it is before 1980 when Tucker began his experiments. The change has not been initiated yet because the machinery to make the change hadn't been invented."

"But the change has already been made," she said again.

"Yes and no," said Jackson. "Or, look at it from another

point of view, we're going to make a change to put history back on the right course. Correct?"

She felt her insides grow cold. Sweat beaded on her forehead and turned her armpits clammy. "Yes," she said.

"Then the books should reflect that change shouldn't they?"

"Yes. I would think so," she said slowly.

"Well, then where is it? The books clearly show that history has taken two diverging paths . . ." Maddie started to speak, but Jackson held up a hand to stop her. "Hear me out," he said.

"If I were to travel from the far future and stop after 1980 but before we initiate our change, then the history books will read one way. If we stop before Tucker invents his machine, or after we made our change, they will read a different way."

"Wait a minute," she said. "I've got you. Those people I talked to at the Alamo left after Tucker invented his machine, yet they knew the right history. I heard one of them express surprise when I said that the Civil War lasted until 1866." She folded her hands across her chest and smiled in triumph.

"No, they left their time before the second change was made. They couldn't be affected by the change because it happened in their future, after they were in the past."

"Jesus Christ in Iaccoca's limousine," she said.

"Yes, but you understand."

"I think so. If we stop in a year after the change but before the invention of time travel, the change hasn't actually been made yet so history is on the right path. If we stop after the invention, and the point of departure for the changer, then we get the new version."

"That's it?"

She shook her head and said, "Talk about wheels inside of wheels."

"It's not nearly as cut and dried as it seems." He laughed. "There used to be a paradox in science-fiction writing that stated you couldn't go back in time to kill your grandfather because if you did, you wouldn't exist to do it."

"Makes sense," she said.

"But it's not true. You can kill your grandfather, especially if your father has already been born, but say that he hasn't. You can still do it because you are the instrument of the change. Without you the change wouldn't have happened. Since it was made, you have to exist. What you might do is wipe out your brothers and sisters, your father or mother, the whole family line after your grandfather, but you won't wipe yourself out."

"I don't think I want to know any more," she said. She cocked her head to one side and then changed her mind. "I do have one other question. What made you look for changes in the past? What tipped you?"

"Just a routine survey," said Jackson. "With the breakthrough that allowed us to send people back and forth without them dying during retrieval, I became concerned about someone making a change without worrying about the consequences. I dropped into 1975 because it was a good base year. I popped into a bookstore and got a copy of a history book. I stopped again in 1990 and got an updated version of the book, and then stopped in 2000 for the last. I just compared them and realized what had happened."

Maddie got to her feet again, stumbled on a stack of books and reached for the door to steady herself. "I'll head back to 1836 in an hour or so," she said. "Drop in a few weeks after my first visit and see what has been decided."

As she opened the door, Jackson said, "I don't think it would be a good idea to go blabbing all over the building what we're doing here. We don't want the Nazis to find out. They might take a dim view of all this since in the history we're trying to return to, they, as a power, ceased to exist in early 1945."

"Not a lot they can do about it," said Maggie. "They're over there in the United States and we have a treaty with them. They won't invade us."

Jackson stood and lowered his voice, as if suddenly frightened. "But they have spies and assassins and if they discovered what was going on, they wouldn't hesitate to kill all of us."

"Oh come on. They're not going to want to kill a couple of scientists," said Maggie.

"Tell that to the people in Auschwitz."

EIGHT

Andross, Kent and Cunningham stepped down from the coach that had brought them from the tiny, dirty train terminal to the downtown of Philadelphia. The journey had taken nearly ten days of riding horseback to the Mississippi, up that river on a great paddle wheeler, to the Ohio and then through a series of canals that connected the Great Lakes, until they reached a hub of the infant railroad system that's main function was to move cargo and passengers from major cities to the canals.

Andross, who stepped down first, was dressed in ragged, dirt smudged buckskins, her long hair tucked up under her cap so that she looked like a boy. Kent and Cunningham were dressed in similar fashion, and had let their hair grow long so that it hung to their shoulders.

When they had their luggage, little more than saddle-bags and clothes wrapped in saddle blankets, they watched the coach drive off in a clatter of shod hooves against cobblestone and a rattle of iron-rimmed wheels.

"Now what?" asked Cunningham, shouldering his saddlebags.

"If the telephone had been invented, I would suggest that we look for Brown's name there. Since that doesn't seem to be a good possibility, I would think that we should find a hotel room, get into clean clothes and then try to find Brown."

"How?" asked Cunningham.

Kent shrugged. "I don't know how. Maybe head to the post office and see if anyone there is familiar with him. Hang around the better restaurants and see if he shows up. Put an ad in the newspaper." He stooped and picked up his gear. "We'll think of something."

"Then let's go," said Andross.

They moved off, along the paved sidewalk. It looked like it was made of brick. Most building fronts were made of brick, stone and wood. Windows were a series of small frames. Those on stores were larger with many panes, some of which were discolored, looking purple in the afternoon sun. The buildings were all fairly small and there were trees and bushes in front of some of them. There was heavy pedestrian traffic, a dozen or so coaches visible, and two street cleaners picking up after the horses. That struck Kent as funny, although he couldn't explain why.

At the corner they stopped, looking right and left. Before they could move, a young man who had been standing with a group of young men stepped forward, jamming his shoulder into Andross's, knocking her to the side.

"Oh, pardon me," he said, smiling. Behind him, his friends were grinning, one of them chuckling.

Andross tried to lower her voice an octave and said, "No problem."

The man stared at her, searching her eyes and looking at the loops of hair that hung from under her hat, unaware that she was a woman. He started to reach out and then let his hand drop. He glanced over his shoulder at his friends as if unsure of what to do.

"Let's go," said Kent, stepping to the side.

The young man turned to face him and then said, "Yes. You had better go. This is my street and you are not welcome on it."

"Then, by all means, we'll get off it as soon as possible," said Cunningham.

The man stood his ground and said, "You misunderstand me. You are not to walk down my street." With that, he reached out and shoved Andross to the side violently. She fell back, to the ground, losing her hat. As her long hair tumbled out, the young man hooted, "Hey! We've found a sissy."

Kent moved then, turning so that his side was facing the man, both hands up, fingers extended and rigid, to protect his face and head. He was up on the balls of his feet, knees flexed, watching the eyes of the man, waiting for him to try something more.

Cunningham put a restraining hand on Kent's arm and said, "It's not worth it."

Now the man smiled and asked, "Your friend unable to defend himself? What you got there? A lily-livered sissy?"

As he stopped speaking, the man threw a punch at Kent's face. Kent ducked his head to the side and snagged the man's fist like he was grabbing a line drive smashed across the infield. As the man jerked his hand to the rear, Kent let go, watching him stumble to the rear.

Two of the other men began to move. Cunningham

watched them spread out and said, "Shit." He dropped his saddlebags. He turned as the men circled, flexing his knees and keeping his hands low. Watching one of them closely, he was aware of the other, suspecting that the beginning of the attack would come from that direction.

The man moved in, swinging a haymaker at Cunningham, but telegraphing the blow. Cunningham dodged to the side, turned his back to the man, stomped down on his instep, and coming back sharply with an elbow, hit the man in the ear.

As that man snapped his hand to his head to cover the pain, Cunningham spun on the second man. Cunningham didn't wait for the attack. He kicked at the man's knee, and heard the crack of bone as the leg broke. The man dropped, his hands on his wound where shards of bone were sticking through the skin and cloth. He shrieked like a wounded rabbit.

The leader of the group went after Kent who blocked a series of jabs easily. When the man threw a punch that turned him slightly, Kent ducked under it and came up with a quick kick to the stomach. The man, surprised and stunned, dropped to his hands and knees, his head hanging down as he tried to suck in air.

Kent held out a hand and tugged Andross to her feet. "You didn't need to do that," she said.

"Well, now we can use the street," said Kent. He crouched, looked at the group's leader, who had rocked back so that he could sit on the ground, his breathing labored. He didn't return the look.

As they moved along the street, Cunningham said, "Now what do we do?"

"I can't see any reason to change our plans. Find a hotel room, get changed and then out to search for Brown and anyone else who might be here."

"You know," said Andross, "this might be a wild-goose chase. We don't know that Brown or any of the others are actually in Philadelphia."

"No," agreed Kent, "but then, Brown said he was coming here and we'll just have to take his word for it."

The search for Brown turned out to be incredibly easy. They split up to cover several different places. Andross headed for the post office, Cunningham said that he would circulate among the restaurants and saloons, and Kent, in a fit of inspiration, said that he would see if the county tax records gave him a clue about Brown.

The search in the assessor's office lasted nearly five minutes. The records, written in a flowing script on a brownish paper, was hard for Kent to read, but the clerk had no trouble. He flipped through the pages, scanning them quickly, until he found an entry that listed a Robert Kevin Brown with an address following it.

He thanked the clerk, a dour man with a pasty complexion who looked like he was about to expire along with his assessor's stamp, and left the office. He walked down the wooden stairs, his footsteps echoing in the hallway, and stepped into the street.

For a moment he stood there, looking at the contrasts. A bustling city with thousands, hundreds of thousands of residents, each going about their task, but not in the laid-back fashion that people of the future believed in. There was a rush, a rat race, but on a different plane because of the modes of transportation and communication. Mail was delivered four times a day, not because the Post Office of 1836 was more efficient, but because it was the quickest way to communicate with people across town. The people of 1836 sent letters the way that people of the future used the telephone.

He stepped into the crowd, almost swept along with it, like a stick in a white-water river. He let himself be dragged along with the mass, watching them. He had thought that Philadelphia in 1836 would be a clean city devoid of air pollution and noise, but found that he was wrong. There was an unmistakable odor of horse in the air and although they didn't have the roar of diesel engines and the squeal of airbrakes, there was a continual din from the horses, the wheeled vehicles, and the people. Live entertainers stood on many corners shouting and singing and playing their instruments. In some respects, the modern city was quieter than the nineteenth century one.

Finally he arrived at the hotel, crossed the wide-open lobby that contained chairs and benches for the patrons. A dozen men dressed in well-made clothes that had little variety to them, or much color, sat around, reading the latest news, including several dispatches from Texas, according to the big headlines. Kent passed them, wished there was an elevator, and then walked up to the fourth floor.

The room was empty. He sat on the bed. A soft thing with a mattress that sagged badly. He opened the window to try to catch the afternoon breeze, but there wasn't one. He took off his shirt and sat in the chair, his arm on the small, round table next to it, and waited.

For the period, the room was ornate. The plastered walls were painted an off-white. There was fancy woodwork around the door and window, and luxurious wooden molding. There were three lamps in the room. One near the bed on a night stand, one on the table and one on the four-drawer dresser near the door. The hardwood floor was polished and partially covered by a woven rug.

A few minutes later, Kent heard Cunningham. He left his room, walked next door and knocked. Cunningham opened the door, smiled and said, "Come on in. You have any luck?"

"Got an address for Brown."

"Must have been quite a trick," said Cunningham. "There must be a thousand Browns in this town."

Kent shrugged. "I just told the clerk that Brown would have arrived only a few weeks ago and five minutes later we had it. Robert Kevin Brown."

"So what do we do now?"

"After Mary Jo returns, I thought we'd drop in on the Colonel and find out if he's happy to see us."

"If I was him," said Cunningham sourly. "I'd be fucking thrilled."

NINE

It was nearly dusk when they arrived at Brown's front door. It was a pleasant house, set close to the street, guarded by a short, ornamental fence of black wrought iron. There was a tiny bit of lawn and several gardens containing a few plants. A couple of early blossoms had appeared.

Kent knocked, waited and knocked again, louder. Brown opened the door a moment later and Kent grinned at him. "Hi, Colonel," he said. "Remember me?"

The expression on Brown's face didn't change. He stepped to the rear, as if inviting Kent to enter and said, "Yes. I remember you."

"Mind if we come in?" asked Cunningham.

Brown opened the door wider and said, "Of course not. Please."

As Kent entered, he saw Thompson standing in the doorway of another room. When she recognized them, she came forward, a smile spreading across her face.

"Welcome," she said. "Welcome."

"Thank you," said Kent. He followed her, the others trailing behind, as she turned and lead him into the parlor. She beckoned to them, gesturing at the chairs.

Brown followed them into the room, almost as if afraid of them. He stopped at the door and leaned against the jamb. He listened as they talked about what had happened to them after they had left the Alamo, about trying to return to the future, and about the arrival of the woman who told them about the problems with history. When Kent described what he had learned about the Civil War, Brown found himself fascinated.

Kent looked at Thompson who sat with both feet flat on the floor, bending forward slightly, as if to hear better. "The woman told us that we are needed to correct the problem in the Civil War. That somehow, our presence in 1836 has created a problem in 1863 and that it is our responsibility to reverse the situation."

Now Brown entered the room and walked to his desk. He leaned on it facing the rest of the group. "I thought that we had agreed that we wouldn't return to the future."

"That was before we knew that our presence in the past would screw up the future," said Kent. "There has been a theory in science fiction that time is like a pond and a stone thrown into it will create ripples throughout it. We were the stone and 1836 was the pond. The changes that manifested themselves in the Civil War are the ripples. Since we created the problem, it is our responsibility to fix it."

"I'll concede that," said Brown. "But first you have to prove to me that a change has taken place in 1863."

"We know now, that the Confederates win the Civil War. That should be proof enough," said Cunningham.

Brown raised a hand and said, "We only have the word of a single woman whom we don't know."

"But she showed us a book that detailed the whole Battle of Gettysburg and there were a number of things that didn't square with what I remember about it."

Brown moved around so that he could sit behind his desk. He propped his elbows on it and leaned his chin on his hands, studying Cunningham and Kent. "In the future, anyone with a computer could produce a book."

"That's not the point," said Kent. "The point is, there has been a change introduced in the Civil War and we have to eradicate it."

"And I'm not convinced that a change has been introduced," said Brown. "If there was a change at Gettysburg, then all the history we remember would have changed with it."

"Now wait a minute," said Kent. "You've lost me."

"Let me see if I can explain it," said Brown. "Now, if the Battle of Gettysburg has been changed by time travelers, wouldn't all the history from that point forward have been changed. Everyone would remember the battle as it now stands, with the change, and never suspect that someone had tampered with time."

"Exactly," said Cunningham. "The newspaper accounts, the diaries, the books, would all reflect the change."

"And everyone who went to school after the change would be taught the new history."

"Agreed," said Kent.

"Then the battle we remember would have to be the new one," said Brown triumphantly.

Kent smiled. "Except that we left the future before the change was introduced in the past and we were therefore unaffected by it."

"But—"

"No buts," said Kent. "We remember history as it was originally played out before there were time travelers messing with history. Now, if there is a change that we don't know about, it means that someone else has entered into the picture, making changes after we left the future. We have to straighten it out."

"They're right," said Thompson. She had been listening to the debate, wanting to return to her home time. Now she had the perfect excuse. "If we caused the problem, we have to fix it."

Brown looked at her and then slowly turned his head so that he could stare at Kent. To Thompson, he said, "You were the one who said that we couldn't play with time. That we had to keep it the way it was. All this came about, our staying in 1836, because you were afraid of what our success would mean to our world."

"But now it's changed anyway and it seems that we're responsible. We have to go put it right. I only objected when it seemed that we were putting unlimited power in the hands of one man or just a few men."

"All right," said Brown. "I'll concede that. But I'm not convinced that this messenger from the future is working with the best interests of everyone in mind."

Kent shifted uneasily in his chair. "We have the book, which disagrees with our memories of the situation."

"But anyone can produce a book," said Brown. "Hell, I remember reading a couple of books about mythical invasions of Japan at the end of the Second World War or what it would have been like had Hitler won the war."

Cunningham felt the blood drain from his face because one of the things that had convinced him of the need to make a change was the fact that Hitler had won the war. He said, "You're suggesting that we have a work of fiction?"

"No," said Brown turning to face him. "I'm suggesting that we can't accept one book as absolute proof that the woman wasn't lying to us."

"She had the letter we sent to Tuck," said Kent.

"So what?" said Brown.

"Look," interjected Cunningham, "this will get us no-where. Can I prove the book isn't fiction? No. Is that important? No. Why not? Because we can go to Gettysburg and see what happens. Look around and if we see an obvious change being made, we can stop it."

Brown shook his head. "How do we know that what we remember is right?"

"Because we were raised on history before anyone could make the changes, therefore it is right," snapped Kent. "All we're saying is that we should look into the situation. If we find we've been lied to, then we don't have to act, but if we don't do it, they'll find someone who will. Someone who might just start making changes to suit his own limited perceptions of how things should be. We won't be able to control that."

Brown was quiet for several moments. The room was filled by the ticking of the clock on the mantle and the sounds of the street drifting on the evening breeze. Finally he said, "If it has been changed, then we must put it back. Now, how do we do that?"

They spent the next hour discussing the way they were going to put the force back together. As Brown had said at the meeting in the Alamo, bright people could find dozens of ways to get rich. All they had to do was scatter across the country and look for opportunities to make a fortune.

"The problem," said Kent, "is that we only have a few days before we have to be back to the Alamo to meet with the woman."

"That's no problem for time travelers," said Brown. "We go meet the woman and then search for our team. Or, better yet, tell her that there will be people meeting her on

June 15, or July 15 and she has to be there. Maybe take her an hour of her time. Could take us months."

Kent clapped his hands together and smiled. "We're supposed to be the ones on the cutting edge here. The ones who can easily think in terms of time. But you're right. We just give out a list of dates to be at the Alamo and see that everyone gets a list. It's beautiful."

Brown stood, glanced at Thompson and said, "Then it's all set. We leave tomorrow as early as possible."

"Why don't you all stay here tonight?" said Thompson.

"All our clothes are at the hotel," said Cunningham.

"That's no problem," said Thompson. "I have something that should fit Mary Jo. I'm sure that we can work something out for the men."

"Then tomorrow, we swing by the hotel before heading for the train station," said Brown.

Kent couldn't help smiling. "You'll love the terminal. They haven't figured out that people will make good cargo. They'll take us, but it's sort of a second-class deal."

"Doesn't matter," said Thompson, "as long as it's the first step in the journey back to our own time."

TEN

Three weeks to the day that they had met with the woman from the future, Kent, Cunningham and Andross, along with Brown and Thompson, were at the Alamo, waiting. They spread out in the chapel courtyard, staring at the crater where the woman had appeared the first time. Since she had arrived at noon, they expected her to return at that time.

It was only a couple of seconds after noon when the bright shimmering started at the chapel doors, making them seem to disappear, the brown coloring the glow until the green of the woman's jumpsuit bled through and the glow faded. As she became a human again, she stepped forward, out of the circle created by the Tucker Transfer, and looked around.

"Is this all of them?" she asked. She looked pointedly at Kent.

"No," said Kent. "We didn't have enough time to round

up everyone. With travel and communication as it is, you're lucky that we could find anyone."

Brown stepped forward and said, "There are some things that we can do, but they'll take time. Of course, if we pop into the future to use modern travel to get us where we're going and then move back into the past, it'll go faster."

The woman smiled as if she was in on some kind of private joke. "Then you shall help us put history back on the right track?"

"We're open to suggestions," said Brown. "But we're going to move with great caution."

"That is to be expected." She reached down and touched her wrist. There was a bracelet around it, looking as if it contained a number of jewels of different colors. She turned then and moved to the chapel doors. "Please, come with me," she said.

She pushed her way past the broken chapel doors and disappeared into the interior. Kent, Cunningham, Andross and the two mercenaries followed. To the left there was a second shimmering and the rapid appearance of a pile of equipment. The woman crouched near it and began plugging cables into a computer terminal and connecting it to a powerpack. Kent bent to help her, grinning at her when she looked at him.

When she finished, there was a large scanning screen set on a couple of vertical rails, a thick cable that ran to the computer that sat on a folding table and a hard-disc drive. There was a keyboard sitting near the monitor. The woman pulled a chair away from the table and sat down.

"There was a problem with Doctor Tucker's machinery, discovered after your journey was initiated. The mapping procedures used were inadequate."

Cunningham moved forward, looked over the woman's

shoulder and watched as she began typing commands into the computer. "Now what in the hell do you mean that the mapping procedures were inadequate?"

She turned and looked at him. "That's not quite accurate. The mapping technique was fine, but the computer used by Tucker was not able to predict the molecular changes in a living organism. During the natural course of living, an organism is undergoing constant change and that change, after something between one and three hours, was significant enough that the retrieval apparatus used by Tucker was unable to cope. When the mapping disagreed with the organic model, the areas of dispute were not retrieved. In other words, portions of the body were left in the past."

"Christ," said Cunningham. "When did Doctor Tucker discover this problem?"

She shrugged. "Before there were any large-scale transfers. In fact, with the exception of yours, there had been no humans traveling until the technology was improved." She smiled, "The solution turned out to be relatively simple. We just had to develop a travel unit small enough to take into the past, with a power source and a computer powerful enough to drive the whole unit."

She waved a hand. "Doctor Tucker didn't have access to this machinery. He needed a much more elaborate set-up for the mapping than is necessary. Now, I can make all the scans, send them into the future and let them make the retrieval within minutes of the scan being completed. Of course, our computers can predict the change in a human body to a much finer degree."

Cunningham shook his head. "We never considered that. The machinery always came back intact. Oh, there was some rust on pieces, but that was it. Never considered all the changes in the body. So the molecules that don't match are left behind."

"That seems to be the problem. Tucker's early experiments produced animals that went into acute distress. Tachycardia arrythmia, shock, cardio-respiratory failure, hepatic failure, renal failure and the like. We think that the molecules were simply left behind causing the collapse of the various body functions that lead to death."

"Jesus. That one is right out of left field. Never even considered it, and now that you mention it, it makes perfect sense."

"So this new mapping," said the woman, "gives our computer the information it needs to force the whole body through the time chute and not cause the trauma experienced by the earlier test animals."

She gestured at the scanner. "If one of you will step behind the screen, we'll get started."

Cunningham moved first. He stood facing them as the screen moved slowly upwards until it hid Cunningham's face, and then slid down until it touched the ground. His body was shown on the screen in a series of glowing and shifting patterns of colored light. Pulsating patterns that were recorded by the computing equipment and written to hard disc.

"Turn around," ordered the woman.

Cunningham faced away and the screen made another pass. When it finished, the woman typed for several minutes and then touched her bracelet again. That done, she rocked back and said, "Before you're recalled, let me tell you a couple of things. First, you'll be taken to a holding room. Stay there and don't move. Read, watch the holovision or listen to the compact system, but don't go out. And second, don't talk to anyone. Not even the technician who'll meet you. This is a secret project and we can't let word of it out. Now, stand over there, near the other room."

"Why do you keep touching your wrist?" asked Kent.

"It tells the people at the far end that we're ready. In a couple of seconds, Mr. Cunningham will be traveling into the future, just as soon as they complete their analysis of the data."

"How does that work?"

"On the same principle as the Tucker Transfer. It's a communication device that allows my people at the far end to receive messages from me."

"Oh."

At that moment, a glow encompassed Cunningham. He took a half-step forward and reached out with a hand, puncturing the bubble of the golden glow. It seemed to creep along his arm until his hand disappeared in it. There was a shimmering as the glow faded and Cunningham disappeared.

The woman smiled and said, "Next."

ELEVEN

The five of them sat in à conference room, around a small table of green plastic. They were in molded plastic chairs that matched the table and the green carpeting on the floor. The walls looked plastic and were painted a lighter green that complemented the table and chairs. There was a pitcher of water and several glasses on the center of the table. Except for a single picture of a city at night, a city hidden in the bright yellowish glow of artificial light and choked with smog, there were no decorations on the walls.

The woman stood at the head of the table, near an open area that looked like an empty jacuzzi. She still wore her emerald jumpsuit, but now was curiously quiet. She kept her eyes on the water, as if expecting it to escape from the table. Occasionally she shot a glance at Kent, letting her eyes slide away when he turned toward her.

A moment later, a man entered, looked around and took

the only open seat. He nodded toward the woman and said, "You may begin, Maddie."

"Thank you, David," she said. "First thing is to determine how to contact the majority of the surviving mercenaries." She looked at Brown but addressed the whole group. "Are there any ideas along those lines?"

"I know," said Brown, "where most of the men and the other women went. It would seem that mail sent general delivery would get to them, eventually. All of us were planning to check the general delivery. Given the plans, I would think that we could find them all. Ads in the newspapers would work too. A couple of them went to New York, one went to Baltimore, places like that."

"And then?" said Jackson.

"Have them assemble somewhere on a specific date and move them to the location you want them."

"It would take only a couple of days, at the most," said Kent, smiling.

"Maddie," said Jackson, "why don't you get a list of who is where from Mr. Brown, and I'll put research on the problem." He looked at Brown and added, "Maybe you could scribble a brief note to them, that we could reproduce. Suggest that they meet at the Alamo chapel on the second of June."

"If I might," said Andross. "Have them meet on the second of several months. Travel times being what they are, some might not make the first date. It wouldn't take much for a time traveler to make a series of one month hops."

"Good idea," said Jackson. "Maddie?"

The woman in the green jumpsuit nodded and made a note on a small pad she held. When Jackson vacated his seat, Maddie slipped into it and whispered to Brown.

While that was going on, Jackson moved to the front and said, "Let's get this show on the road." He turned to the side and waved his hand at an area of the wall. The lights dimmed slightly and there was a series of flashes from the jacuzzi.

"If you'll direct your attention to the holograph tank, I'll give you an overview of the problem." Jackson looked at Brown as he finished dictating his message, and added, "As a military leader, you're probably more familiar with this conflict than anyone in the room, including me. And please remember that my briefing will be colored by the influences of the time changes introduced by the unknown.

As the light show popped a couple of times and then solidified into a representation of the landscape around Gettysburg, Maddie left the room. Kent watched her go and then joined the others who had turned their attention to a group of blue boxes formed along the high ground, running from Little Round Top on the south, northward toward the town until it bent back to the south on Culp's Hill, so that the Union line looked like a fishhook. Gray boxes snapped into existence forming lines facing the blue.

"This is the relative postion of the various forces at Gettysburg on the second day. It was the second day's fighting that set the tone for the rest of the battle and what happened on the third. The important point," said Jackson pushing his hand at the display, "is that neither side seemed to believe that the first thing to do was take the high ground. It wasn't until late in the day that they, meaning both sides, tried to take the Round Tops. In the history we need to attain, the Union won the race and secured that portion of their lines."

"The ground there is very rough," said Brown, "which meant that a small group of Federal soldiers was able to prevent the rebels from taking it."

"And they were quickly reinforced," said Jackson, "by the Union."

"Right."

"Now, in the rewritten version of history, someone has told the Rebels that they need to take the Round Tops, so at noon, a large force, under Longstreet, sallies from the main Confederate lines and storms the hills. The Union response is slow in developing and is repulsed."

Jackson looked at Brown and then swung his gaze over the others. "That meant that the Union flank was not securely anchored, although a large force, under the Union generals Sykes and Sedgwick, could keep the Rebels from pursuing their gains."

Brown stood and moved closer to the tank where he could see the new developments outlined in blue and gray lights, small rectangles with Xs on the tops that indicated the size of the unit. He noticed the shift in the lines and saw the weakness now evident.

"So now," said Brown, "when Pickett, Trimble and Pettigrew launched their attack at the center of the Union lines on the third day, they received support from the Round Tops, forcing the Union to withdraw to the north and east and opening everything up."

Jackson grinned at Brown. "How do you stop that?"

"Easy. Put a group of sharpshooters on Big Round Top and let them keep the Rebels from taking either it or Little Round Top. Get someone on the Union side to realize the importance of that high ground so that they'll have someone on it when the Rebels try to take it, and history goes back to the way it was."

"That easy?" asked Jackson.

Brown rubbed a hand under his chin, studying the display. "Maybe not quite that easy. You'll need someone who understands enough about military tactics and strategies that he'll be able to evaluate the action on the field and respond to it. And he'll need a force large enough to stop Longstreet, if Longstreet decides to commit a major part of his corps to the attack."

"So what do you need?" asked Jackson.

"A heavy weapons squad," replied Brown. "Fifteen, twenty men, armed with automatic weapons, supported by grenadiers and mortars. Maybe recoilless rifles. From Big Round Top, we could stop any initial assault made by the rebels. Give the Union time to put someone on the hill. And one or two men to act as scouts to tell someone on the Union side to get help up the hill."

"Who would that be?" asked Jackson, his eyes focused on the holographic display.

"If you mean who would be the scouts, that could be anyone who would be credible to the Union chain of command. If you mean who would we go to for help, probably General Gouverneur Warren since he is responsible for securing that ground, according to the history I know."

"Is there any special training that you'll need," asked Jackson.

"I don't know what it would be," said Brown. "My people all know their jobs, or what their jobs were. It's a simple holding action." He turned and looked at Kent, Cunningham and Andross. "There is nothing for these people to do." He realized how that sounded and tried to soften it. "They're scientists and not soldiers."

"Wait a minute," snapped Kent. "You can't leave us out of this. We might not be soldiers in the sense that we aren't trained mercenaries like you, but we were at the Alamo with you and did a good job of covering your back. Besides, you need someone there versed in the ramifications of time travel. We can spot trends that you might not. Your job is fighting. Ours would be protecting the fabric of time."

"Mr. Kent has a point," said Jackson.

"More than one," agreed Brown. "He's right about the help they provided at the Alamo." He turned his attention to them. "I merely meant that it wasn't necessary for you to go on this one."

"Understood," said Cunningham.

"So, when can you leave," asked Jackson.

"Just as soon as my team is assembled, and that's up to you."

TWELVE

Before returning to the flophouse where he could have a
bed for a nickel a day, Lemuel Crawford stopped at the
local post office. He stood quietly in line, listening to the
pop of the gaslights and waited for his turn. He felt bone-
tired, having worked fourteen hours that day, digging a
trench with five other men for their bonus of a dollar.

His pay was only a dollar a day and from that he had to
buy a place to sleep and food to eat. It didn't give him
much chance to save anything.

He was aware of his own body odor, but then most
everyone there had the same problem. Baths cost money
and with the expense of living from day to day, he didn't
have much extra to spend on luxuries like baths and hair-
cuts.

Finally he was at the front of the line and gave the clerk
his name. The man returned with a single envelope and
when Crawford saw it, he knew who it was from. He

didn't have to see the return address. He slipped from the lobby into the area where the boxes were. He moved to the window where the last light of the dying sun was pouring through. As he ripped open the envelope, he realized that the note was from the future. He didn't have to read the message to know that. In 1836 there were no Xerox machines and the message was a Xerox copy. Those standing around him wouldn't recognize it because they had never seen one, but Crawford knew.

He read it quickly and nodded to himself. "Yeah," he said, and felt a bubbling of excitement in the pit of his stomach. An excitement because he had worked in his last trench, sweating and straining for a buck that would almost cover the day's living expenses. An excitement because now there was a goal in the near future. He didn't know if he could make the Alamo by June 2nd, given the problems of traveling across country without benefit of railroads and automobiles, but it didn't matter. There was a second pickup scheduled for the second of July.

If he hurried, he might make the earlier pickup. A swing by the flophouse for his belongings, which consisted of a couple of shirts and an extra pair of pants. He could be on the road by ten and with luck, to the Alamo in two weeks. If he got the breaks.

He folded the letter back into the envelope and stepped into the street. Suddenly everything looked better to him. Suddenly life was better. In just a very few weeks, he would be home.

Peter James Baily sat at the table covered with a green felt cloth, shuffling the cards. A tall, thin man with neatly trimmed hair slicked back, dark eyes and a large, flowing moustache, he was becoming a dandy. To his left was a pile of chips worth nearly seven hundred dollars. He had already cashed in enough chips to put a thousand into the various pockets of his suit. He could feel the comforting weight of a pepperbox derringer in his vest and knew, although he couldn't feel, the letter in the inside pocket of his coat.

Baily handed the cards to the left to be cut and began to deal slowly. His mind was no longer on the game, but back in the Alamo, in the dim, musty-smelling room in the long barracks with Brown in the front telling them that they had to stay in the past. Had to stay in 1836 to prevent Lewis and his corporate boys from winning. To keep them from gaining unlimited power.

Baily picked up his hand and looked at his cards, sorted them slowly, carefully so that he didn't give anything away and laid them face down on the table. He let someone else open, called and waited.

If Brown was now trying to reassemble the team, it meant that something had changed. Something that would let them return to the future where they belonged. He had done all right in the past. Parlayed his thousand into near ten, but he had done it with cards and gambling and not with clever investments. Not the way he had planned, but the way it had worked.

Baily ran a hand through his longish blond hair and tossed his money into the pot. He picked up his cards and looked at them again. He suddenly felt sick to his stomach as the three of diamonds turned into the three of hearts and he realized that his flush had collapsed. He didn't even have a pair, having tossed in the black ten when he drew his cards.

As the winner scooped his chips from the center of the table, Baily stood and said, "Thank you, gentlemen, but I think that will be all for tonight."

"Leavin' winners," said one of the men.

"For tonight," said Baily, again aware of the derringer.

"Maybe we'd like a chance to get our money back," said the man, sliding his chair to the rear.

Baily stood his ground, staring into the man's eyes and said, "Look, you're having a bad run tonight. When you hit the bad streak, you quit for a while. Come back later, the next day and look for the good streak. Tomorrow you can have your chance to get your money back." Baily put all the sincerity he could into the smile.

"Makes good sense, Jason," said one of the other men. "Makes real good sense."

Jason fingered the button of his coat and stared at his feet. Finally he dropped into his chair and said, "Yes. Makes good sense. Tomorrow then, and I'll bring the cards."

"New deck," said Baily. "Brand new and I'll be happy to use your cards."

"You be here tomorrow," said Jason. "And bring plenty of money."

"Don't worry about that," answered Baily. "Gentlemen, until tomorrow." He walked out, turned and headed for the docks. By the next evening, he hoped to be well down the river, getting closer to Texas and the Alamo.

Meg Clark sat on the steps waiting for Summers to get home. She had gone to the post office and picked up the mail. She hadn't opened the letter until she had gotten home, but the moment she pulled the sheet from the envelope, she knew what it was. She had read the message rapidly, packed quickly, and then sat on the steps where she could watch the front door, waiting for Summers.

When she saw the knob turning, she was on her feet, grinning. As Summers entered, she said, "The decision has been taken from us."

"Yes," said Summers ignoring her. "Welcome home, Bill. Have a nice day, Bill?"

"Sorry," she said, "but this came today." She waved the letter like it was some kind of a flag. "Letter from Brown."

Summers pushed the door shut and dropped the books he was carrying on the table near the door. "What did the Colonel say?" He reached out and said, "Give it here."

Quickly, he scanned the sheet, saw the suitcases sitting near the wall and said, "I know what your answer is. You want to go. You sure this is a good idea?"

Clark shrugged. "It's the Colonel telling us that we have something more to do. What could be wrong with it? Yes, I think we should go."

Summers hesitated, wanted to move into another room to talk, but stood with his back to the door. "How do you know it comes from the Colonel?"

"If it doesn't, what have we lost? We take a trip to Texas and see how things have progressed. No big deal."

Summers pulled the hat from his head and stared at her. He had spent the day in conference with a number of men, wheeling and dealing, pretending that he was in his own time. There had been no interruptions by telephones, no annoying Muzak in the background, and no mind-numbing jet roars overhead. Only the ticking of a clock in the corner that somehow reminded him that time was passing. Lunch had been brought in by a number of male secretaries. The windows had been opened, letting in the warm, afternoon breezes, but for those things, he could easily have been conducting his business in 1985.

But, he knew how Meg felt about 1836 and he couldn't blame her. He moved to the steps and sat down beside her, draping an arm over her shoulders. "I guess there is nothing going on here that I couldn't leave for a while. Give me tomorrow to clean up the business and then we'll see about getting to Texas."

"You mean it?" she asked happily.

"Sure," he said. "Why not?"

Steve Dennison sat at the desk in his room, the notes he had made the night before in a neat pile in front of him. He had spent the morning outlining the battle of Vicksburg, trying to remember everything he could about the siege. That finished, he had made his way to the post office, something he did on the off chance that someone wrote to him. Now he had Brown's letter and wasn't sure what to do with it.

He read the letter again. It told him nothing that he needed to know. Only that Brown had found them another mission somehow and he was requesting that they all meet at the Alamo on June 2nd. It was the last thing that Dennison wanted to do. Meet at the Alamo. He had his life for the next twenty-five years mapped out, and he didn't want to do anything to undermine that.

He let the letter fall to the desk top and walked to the window so that he could look out on the street. He felt sweat beading on his forehead and wiped it away with one hand. He pushed open the window and let the sounds of the street, of the children, blow up to him. Two black men were loading boxes on a wagon while a white man sat in the shade watching them.

Slavery wasn't the real issue of the Civil War, Dennison told himself. It was states' rights. Could the federal government force the individual states to do things, to pass laws that the local population felt were wrong? He remembered the government forcing the states in the 1980s to pass a 55 miles an hour speed limit and mandatory seatbelt law, but unable to force the motor companies to install airbags. The Civil War had given the feds the right to tell the states what to do, but not business.

And slavery would have died out as it became economically inefficient. When machinery could do the job easier and cheaper, the issue of slavery would have died a natural death. Maybe it was good that it ended in the Civil War. One moment there were slaves and the next it was illegal to own them. It prevented a lingering death that could have caused a great number of social problems.

But, as Dennison stood there, he realized that slavery and states' rights were not the issues that concerned him. It was the preservation of the South. He just couldn't stand by and let the North win again. He could not stand by while Sherman and his bandits marched to the sea, burning everything behind them. Not when he knew every mistake that a Southern leadership would make during the war. Not when he could prevent it.

He stepped back to his desk and picked up the letter. He read it a final time. There was really nothing in it that affected him. Slowly he crumpled the paper into a tight ball and cocked his arm to throw it. Then he stopped, dug in his pocket for a match, and scratched his thumb across it. He touched the flame to the paper, held it as it burned and then dropped it into the ashtray sitting near his maps.

"I never got the message, Colonel," he said. "Never got it at all."

THIRTEEN

When Jackson and Brown finished their discussion of the Battle of Gettysburg, the lights in the holographic tank winked out and Jackson said, "We'll need to get you down to wardrobe for fittings and then into the main conference room for a thorough briefing."

"Wardrobe?" said Thompson.

"Of course," said Jackson. "You can't be sent into 1863 Pennsylvania dressed as 1836 frontiersmen. You'll have to be in proper uniforms for your story to be credible."

"We didn't need wardrobe last time," said Brown.

"No, but the situation was somewhat different," said Jackson. "We now want you to drop into 1863 without creating a disturbance. If you're dressed in the proper clothing, you'll be less likely to cause a ripple."

"Our weapons," said Brown. "They'll stick out."

Jackson smiled at that. "We've had some assistance from a couple of other divisions and they have provided us with weapons that look like those being used in 1863, but modified for semi-automatic and fully automatic fire."

"There are questions," said Kent.

"Yes, I imagine there are," responded Jackson. "But it's not important to answer them now. Anything that you want to know will be covered in the full briefing before transport to the proper time coordinates."

"The assumption being that we're going along with this plan of yours," said Cunningham.

Jackson turned so that he faced Cunningham. "Why wouldn't you go along? We're not attempting to change time, just put it back the way it's supposed to be. What's the problem?"

Now Cunningham looked at the others, as if wanting one of them to take over. When no one spoke, Cunningham said, "You're pushing too hard. You've given us no time to review the data or to ask any tough questions. Every time we come up with one, you dodge it by saying we'll get the answer in some other briefing."

"There are schedules to maintain," said Jackson.

"We have no schedules," responded Cunningham. "We have questions but no schedules."

"Gentlemen. Ladies," said Jackson. "I assure you that all your questions will be answered, but while you're in that briefing, it would be beneficial for us to be readying your costumes."

"The assumption still being that we'll be going on the mission," said Brown.

Jackson shrugged. "Listen to what we have to say and analyze it. Relate it to what you already know and when you see that all we want to do is put history back on its proper course, I'm sure that you'll accept the mission."

"If you can answer one question for us," said Cunningham. "Why don't you just take care of it yourself?"

Jackson rubbed a hand through his hair and then wiped his palm on the front of his jumpsuit. "You've already been broken loose from the time stream, so to speak. And you've had some experience working in the past. Those are two very good reasons to use you. Now, please, let's head for wardrobe."

Jackson talked as if they had a vast empire of time-traveling agents and sections, and wardrobe was a large, brightly lighted room stuffed with racks of clothes, bolts of cloth, tables, tailor's dummies, sewing machines and thousands of scissors, needles, spools of thread, tapes and the like. A woman, looking like she had escaped from central casting in the part of a tailor, waved them in. She was a short woman, plump, wearing a khaki coat with needles stuck in the lapels, a tape about the neck, scissors jammed in her pockets and a handful of cloth clutched under her arm.

She spit pins out of her mouth and waved. "Come on. Come on. We're behind schedule." She stared at Jackson and said, "These the Civil War people?"

"Yes," said Jackson. He was trying to angle them toward a rack containing the dark blue coats and sky blue trousers of the Union Army.

The woman caught his arm and spun him toward the door. "You just get out of here. We'll handle this. I'll have them down to you in a few minutes."

As Jackson turned, a group of three women and two men seemed to appear from no where. They propelled Brown and his mercenaries toward the Civil War uniforms, each figuring sizes and seizing coats from the racks.

One of the men handed a jacket to Brown and said, "Will you be leading the party?"

Brown looked at him, then at Thompson who stood

there smiling. The three former assistants to Tucker stood to one side but didn't speak. "Yes," said Brown. "I will be the leader."

"Ah," said the man. "Presented us with some problems. Had trouble deciding what rank to assign. Too high and there would be questions about who you were and too low and some captain or major might order you off the Round Top."

"For a tailor, you seem extraordinarily well versed in the mission," said Brown.

"We're a small operation and while I assist in the wardrobe duties, my first job lies elsewhere." He stared up at Brown and then said, "We've decided to make you a colonel. There were enough regiments running around that no one could keep track of all the colonels."

Brown took the jacket handed to him and tried it on. He didn't like it. The material was rough, ill-cut and badly dyed. He was handed a pair of pants that had buttons on the fly rather than a zipper. These were not made of the same material as his own Army dress uniform left in the future or in the past. In his home time. He turned, saw the others trying on their clothing, the women ignoring the men around them.

"This is going to be hot for July in Pennsylvania."

"Can't be helped," said the man. "The design is from the period, but the material isn't exactly right. No one looking at it will be able to tell a thing about it, but if you'll look carefully, you'll see that we've woven kevlar into it to make it bullet resistant."

"Bullet *resistant?*" repeated Brown. He didn't like the sound of that.

"Yes. It'll stop a pistol slug from fairly close range and should stop most rifle or musket fire from a couple of meters. At extremely close range you're going to get some penetration."

"Great."

"Now," said the man, "if you'll slip on the trousers, we'll see what we have to do them."

An hour later, Brown and company were lead into the main conference room. Each person was carrying the modified weapons that Jackson had told them about. Most were modeled after Enfield 1855 carbines or Enfield 1855 rifles, and designed to hold twenty rounds concealed under the barrel. Loading them was like loading a modern pump-shotgun. The rounds were jammed up from the bottom, but a gas chamber worked the bolt. Close examination by a soldier would reveal the design differences, but as long as the mercenaries stayed away from the regular troops, no one should spot the differences.

They were asked to leave their weapons outside the conference room, in racks already filled with muskets and rifles. As they entered, Brown stopped short and looked at the assembled men. He recognized them immediately. He took a step toward them, waved a hand at Pete Baily and Bob Crossman. Sitting across from them was Meg Clark and Bill Summers.

Brown glanced back at Thompson and leaned close to her. "Good, I see they've found McGee. I was hoping he would be one of them."

As they moved in, Brown spotted a couple of others. John Blair, Tom Waters and John Forsyth. He wanted to say something to them, but it had been only a few weeks since all of them had ridden out of the Alamo. It wasn't like it had been months since the last meeting. As he started toward them, Jackson coughed once as if to signal he wanted to begin.

Jackson stood at the front, on a slightly raised platform, trying to look important. He waved them into the room and said, "I guess you all know one another, so I won't make any introductions."

"You sure put this together quickly," said Brown, genuinely impressed.

"Not really," said Jackson. He laughed and then added, "You forget that we've got time travel. Once we had everyone retrieved that we could get, everyone who made either of the dates at the Alamo, we brought them to our time, briefed them, took them to wardrobe and then brought them to this time. Weeks of work for us. An hour or so for you."

Brown sat down without another word and looked at the last two people. Mark Sewell and John Cane. He realized that some of the survivors of the Alamo were missing. Issac Millsaps was one, but then Millsaps had been the corporate representative and would be of no help in the upcoming assignment. He didn't see Sam Holloway or Bob Cochran. Both of them had talked about going to California and since that meant a trip across the plains where the Indians still ruled, it could mean they were dead. Although the Plains Indians wouldn't be fighting heavily for another decade or so. Wouldn't be fighting until they realized that the trickle of white men and women would soon turn to a flood. And then they would fight, not realizing that it was too late to stop them. That it had been too late when the first immigrants made the trek west.

And there were one or two others he didn't see. Steve Dennison, a southerner from Texas, wasn't there. Neither was Bill Dearduff. That didn't mean much.

Brown slumped into the theaterlike seats, the back of his head resting on the top of the chair, his knees against the one in front of him, and waited. Waited for Jackson to tell them once again what they would have to do.

In that moment, Brown realized that he was going to do whatever was asked of him. He didn't need to see another briefing on the matter, or hear arguments about what had to be done to correct time. He had decided to do it when the man had started fitting him with his uniform. He had decided that it was something that had to be done.

Jackson looked out at the people there, seemed to be waiting for them to fall silent and then began once again. Explaining all the problems with history and how a single change in 1863 should put history back on the proper path. He outlined all the changes made after the initial one and then added, "And one last thing we have to be aware of. George Custer, in command of the Michigan brigade of cavalry at Gettysburg, was killed late in the third day by a sniper. We have to ensure that it doesn't happen because he has to die at the Little Big Horn thirteen years later."

From that point there were questions and answers. Then more questions and answers until they were discussing the same thing over and over again. Talking about possibilities that had a chance of occurring, talking about contingencies in case something else happened, talking about the Round Tops, and Culp's Hill and Pickett's Charge until it was all boring and time consuming.

Brown got to his feet, waited until everyone fell silent and asked, "How soon are we going to be sent back?"

Jackson looked out at the group, stood quietly, rocking back and forth on his heels and said, "Just as soon as you can get into your uniforms and pick up your weapons. We'll head to the master control and get the machinery warmed up. You could be gone in twenty minutes."

FOURTEEN

Steven Dennison had waited twenty-seven years for this moment. He had spent his time wishing that he had studied the Civil War era of American history with more of an eye to detail. He had spent the last twenty-seven years in Atlanta, trying to put together a history of the War Between the States so that he would be ready when it finally happened. Now he was in southern Pennsylvania, in 1863, about to give Robert E. Lee everything he needed to win the upcoming battle and the war.

The ride had been hard, through country that was alive with troops from both sides. Stuart and his cavalry off on a mission for Lee. Union Generals Hooker and then Meade, staying between Stuart and a quick route to Washington. Lee and the Army of Virginia marching north to take the war to the Union. Each side suspicious of lone men of military age who didn't wear a uniform.

But Dennison had no trouble. He was stopped by the

pickets of Lee's army. Tired, dirty men with three-days growth of beard on their faces and black circles under their eyes, armed with outdated rifles. They escorted Dennison to a farmhouse surrounded by tents. A Confederate sergeant took him to the house, knocked on a door that bled light through gaps in the boards, and then stood aside as an officer opened it.

"Man claims to have important information," the sergeant told the officer.

The officer looked at Dennison who, like the sentries who had stopped him, was tired and dirty. His coat was ripped and his trousers were tattered. He had been carrying a Colt revolver that the sentries had taken and given to the sergeant, who now held it out for the officer.

"Who are you," demanded the officer.

Dennison hesitated, afraid to give his real name. He didn't know why he was afraid, it was just a feeling in the back of his mind that somehow Brown, or one of the other mercenaries would be at Gettysburg and know what he had done. So, he looked into the eyes of the officer and said, "Harrison. With information of great importance to the command of this army."

The officer glanced at the revolver, took it from the sergeant and then stood back. "Enter," he said to Dennison. Then to the sergeant, "You may return to your post."

"Yes sir," said the sergeant as he disappeared.

The officer closed the door and said, "You wait right here. Don't move and don't touch anything. You got that?"

"Yes."

"I'll be right back." He turned and moved toward the table that was set in the middle of the room. There were a number of officers around it studying a large map that covered it like a Sunday tablecloth. Two lamps, their wicks turned high, burned at the corners of the table, throwing a

bright glare and sending two thick, black columns of soot
at the ceiling. Another officer sat at a small desk, a lamp in
front of him, writing something with a quill pen, the
scratching audible across the room.

The officer stepped close to one of the men at the map
table and said, quietly, "Major Sorrel, there is a man here
who claims to have knowledge of the Union troop movements."

The Major stood up, glanced at his maps and then
crossed the room. He held out a hand and said, "I'm Major
Sorrel of General Longstreet's staff."

"Good evening, Major," said Dennison. "I'm Harrison
from Mississippi. I have some intelligence that might
prove useful."

"About Hooker's armies?"

"No sir. General Hooker has quit. General Meade has
replaced him."

Sorrel raised his eyebrows in question.

"Just happened. Hooker wanted more troops and said
that if he didn't get them, he'd quit. His resignation was
accepted and General Meade was placed in command of
the Army of the Potomac."

Now Sorrel smiled. "That is good news."

"Why?" asked Dennison.

"Because they're replacing their commander and it will
take him time to get the feel of the job. There should be a
month, two month's transition time. Gives us an advantage
and we haven't had to fire a shot."

"Then I have more good news," said Dennison.

Sorrel put a hand on Dennison's shoulder and said,
"Come on over to the maps and tell us what you've seen."

When Dennison finished talking about the placement of
the Union forces and the directions in which they were

driving, Sorrel said, "I think the General will want to see this. Come with me."

At the door, they stopped and Sorrel looked toward the table with the maps on it. He saw the pistol taken from Harrison there and went to retrieve it. As he handed it to the man, he said, "I don't think we need to keep this."

Dennison accepted it gratefully and stuck it into the thin, leather holster fastened to his belt. It was not the fancy, quick-draw holster tied to his thigh that had been popularized by the gunmen of Hollywood movies, but a long, leather sheath that hid and protected everything but the grip that was just barely visible.

"Thanks," said Dennison.

Outside, Sorrel ordered two horses and in moments a corporal appeared leading them. Sorrel mounted and said, "It's not far to General Longstreet's camp."

They rode down a narrow path, just a brown slash in the green of the fields, passed a rail fence and around a clump of elm and cedar trees. At the top of a slight rise, barely visible against the dark sky that was ablaze with stars, Dennison could see another farmhouse. The windows stood out, bright squares of yellow marking the spot.

As they approached, they were challenged by the guards, one man's accent so thick that he was nearly impossible to understand. Sorrel leaned close so that the soldier, his weapon tipped with a bayonet, could see his face and said, "I'll be wanting to speak with General Longstreet."

The guard hesitated and then told them to proceed. At the front of the house, a stone structure two stories tall with a wide chimney at each side, they climbed off their horses. Sorrel let the reins fall to the ground and the horse drifted to the right where there was tall, green grass. Sorrel stepped onto the covered porch, the leather of his boots

echoing hollowly as he moved to the door. He rapped on it
and then grabbed the knob, twisting.

Dennison followed, entering a foyer where a sergeant
sat. He looked up and said, "Kin ah hep y'all, sur?"

Sorrel stared down at him and said, "Chief of staff?"

The sergeant got slowly to his feet and opened a door
that lead into the library. "This way, sur."

Inside Dennison was introduced to the men, Sorrel
using the name Harrison for him. Once again, Dennison
told the men what he knew and what he suspected of the
Union Army's intentions. Each listened carefully and when
Dennison was finished, one of the men, a colonel, said that
he was going to awaken the General.

"He'll want a full report."

And ten minutes later, Dennison was again explaining
about the replacement of Hooker and the distribution of the
Union forces. Longstreet listened gravely sitting in a large,
wing-back chair, one hand propping up his head as if he
was about to fall asleep again.

When Dennison finished, Longstreet got up and said, "I
want this man sent to General Lee's headquarters now.
Major Sorrel, you'll escort him."

Within an hour, the thin red glow of dawn marking the
horizon to the east, Sorrel and Dennison pulled up in front
of Lee's headquarters, a small, single-story building that
was dark. Again the guards challenged them, finally al-
lowing them to proceed. The Duty Officer, Lieutenant
Randolph McKim, met them at the door and took them
inside. Sorrel ordered him to wake Lee, which the Lieutenant was reluctant to do, saying that, "General Lee just
went to bed."

"This is of extreme importance," said Sorrel. "You have
your orders, Lieutenant."

McKim left the room and returned a few minutes later. He said, "General Lee will be with you in just a moment."

Unlike Longstreet, Lee came in wearing a complete uniform and looking as if he had just spent a restful night. He nodded at Sorrel and greeted him by name. He stared at Sorrel's uniform, now dirty and wrinkled. He glanced down at the boots that were black, but not polished. He said nothing about this.

Sorrel bowed slightly and said, "General, may I present Mister Harrison of Mississippi. He has brought us some intelligence of importance."

Lee came forward and held out a hand. "Mister Harrison."

Dennison shook Lee's hand and suddenly felt something stir in his gut. He couldn't identify what it was. Maybe just excitement at meeting a man he had read and heard about all his life. A man who had taken on the stature of the ages now stood in front of him. A gray-haired man with a neat gray beard who seemed to be no taller than average. A man who seemed no greater than average, but who symbolized the Southern Aristocracy.

"The pleasure is mine, sir," said Dennison, aware of the awe that had crept into his voice.

"Please, be seated," said Lee. "Tell me what you have learned."

So again Dennison outlined what he knew of the Union movements. His memory of the events, colored by the years and the historians' perspectives, left a few narrow gaps in his knowledge, and it may have been those gaps that convinced Lee of the truth of what Dennison was saying. It wasn't perfect information, but it sounded very good.

When Dennison finished, Lee rose to his feet and shook

hands again, thanking Dennison for the information. "You don't know how valuable this intelligence is," he said.

Together, Sorrel and Dennison moved to the door. As they left, Dennison heard Lee telling McKim that he wanted to see Generals Longstreet and Hill quickly. Their orders were to be changed. Instead of Harrisburg, they were to head to Gettysburg to try to intercept the Union Army.

FIFTEEN

The men and three women assembled in the transfer chamber, a bowl-shaped room, standing on a plastic floor and looking at the plastic walls. Fifteen feet up on one wall was a wide window, behind it Brown could make out the faces of several technicians as they worked. There was nothing else in the room visible behind the glass. Even the door through which they had entered seemed to have disappeared.

As Brown turned to inspect his troops, all of them, including the women, outfitted as members of a cavalry regiment, the golden glow of time travel seemed to descend on them. Brown was aware of the trip starting, a dizzying sensation like standing in a glassed elevator and seeing another one take off. He reached out toward the wall as it shimmered and disappeared, and the passing days took on the qualities of an erratic strobe.

All at once they stopped, the air of the early July morning in southern Pennsylvania washing over them. There wasn't a sudden sensation of the trip ending, just the realization that they were no longer moving. Brown blinked in the bright sunlight, felt sweat bead on his forehead and wiped his sleeve across it. The men and women still stood in the same positions they had held when the trip started, although a couple were wavering as if they were about to collapse.

Brown dropped to one knee and surveyed his surroundings. To the right, west of where they stood, not more than a hundred meters away, was the edge of a town. Brown hoped that it was Gettysburg. There was a road behind them to the north and a stream to the south. Somewhere to the east was supposed to be a cavalry brigade that might have already made contact with the Rebels. He wondered what time it was. Judging from the sun, it seemed that it was about seven in the morning.

Around them, nothing was moving. Brown thought that he should take his people to the south. There was a single Union division there, holding some of the high ground. On the first day, it wouldn't be that important, at least from Brown's point of view. It wasn't until the second day that Brown had to worry about anything.

Firing erupted in the west. Sporadic firing, drifting toward them on the light breeze. Most of the men dropped to the ground, searching the surrounding countryside with their eyes, but they could see nothing. Brown stood upright, his eyes scanning the horizon to the west.

"What's happening, Bob?" asked Thompson.

"Union and Rebels are skirmishing along the Chambersburg Pike," said Brown. "That's to the west of the town."

Kent crawled up, trying to keep his head below the top

of the tall, dusty grass. He crouched near Brown, his rifle clutched in his left hand. "What do we do now?"

"Firing's a good two miles from us," said Brown, looking down on the man. "It'll shift to the east slowly, with the Union taking up positions on McPhersons's Ridge in the beginning. Later they'll fall back, giving those positions to the Rebels, forming their lines on Seminary Ridge. If we move out now, we'll have nearly all day to get to the Round Tops and we can keep two ridge lines between us and the fighting."

"How far is it?"

Brown turned and pointed. "It's beyond those hills there, maybe three miles, maybe less. Even at a fairly leisurely pace, we can be there in a couple of hours."

Kent looked up at Brown and slowly got to his feet. In the distance there was still the sound of firing. Sometimes it grew heavy, the individual reports merging into a single, drawn-out concussion. The sound would rise and fall as the opposing forces jockeyed for position.

"I don't know about this," said Kent.

Brown turned and looked him in the eye. "What don't you know about this?"

"They've maneuvered us and pushed us and given us no time to think about it," said Kent. "Those briefings weren't all that complete."

Now Brown smiled. "I've listened to you and your two friends argue theories of time travel for the last few days. I listened to that discussion you had with Jessie. I didn't understand much of it, except to learn there are two paths for history, and the one the world finds itself on is wrong. But now we're back into my element. I can tell you everything that is going to happen for the next three days."

"Such as," said Kent.

"Such as at about ten-thirty, ten-forty-five, the Union general in command is going to get picked off. That command will fall to Abner Doubleday—yes, the baseball guy. By the end of the day, both armies will be committed to a battle that neither really wants. Tomorrow, about four o'clock, our role becomes crucial because that will be when both sides decide that the high ground of the Round Tops should be taken. Except that we'll be there to keep the Rebels off it. History will return to the normal path."

Kent looked at the open ground around them. Fifteen, twenty men, and three women dressed like the men, crouching in the early morning sun, waiting for someone to give them orders. Twenty people, who, if found by a Rebel force of any size, could be exterminated quickly. Yet, here they sat, discussing theories of time travel and tactics of war.

"Maybe we should get out of the open," said Kent.

Brown shook his head. "Not that necessary. Everything is going on to the west of Gettysburg right now. Closest enemy unit would probably be a division under the command of Jubal Early, but they won't be in sight for a couple of hours."

Kent was going to say something to that. And to say that they had an interesting opportunity to study the workings of time. They had, in essence, two missions. Save the Union at Gettysburg, and then save Custer at Hanover. If they completed the first mission, then they probably wouldn't have to worry about the second. It would take care of itself.

But, he didn't say any of that to Brown. He just waited, hoping that Brown would decide to get them away from the town of Gettysburg, if it was Gettysburg. He had seen nothing to convince him that they were even in the right place, although Brown seemed satisfied that they were.

Finally Brown, squinting in the sunlight, said, "Let's get into position. We've got plenty of time, and this way we'll have the opportunity to watch the development of the battle. See history being made."

SIXTEEN

Maddie sat in Jackson's office flipping through a history book, studying the action at Gettysburg as it should have unfolded, and waited. She had told Jackson that she should accompany the mercenaries to 1863 and Jackson had over-ruled her. She had explained the importance of having someone with a knowledge of the different history of Gettysburg with the mercenaries, and Jackson had disagreed. Finally she had just demanded that she be sent with them because someone had to watch out for their interests and Jackson had said, "No!"

A moment later Jackson opened his door, stopped and looked at her. "What the hell are you made up for?"

She glanced at herself. The dark blue coat, made of the same bullet-resistant material as that of the mercenaries, hung on her, concealing her shape. The sky blue trousers were baggy and the black boots loose. Her brown hair was

92

piled on the top of her head so that she could hide it under the campaign hat that sat on the floor next to her.

"I'm ready to be employed on this mission," she said smiling.

Jackson walked around her and sat behind his desk. "I thought that we had settled that an hour ago. You're not going. No need for you to go."

"David," she said, "you're flat out wrong on this. The briefings we've provided are woefully inadequate. True, Brown has a good knowledge of the battle, but he hasn't studied it in years. He's aware of how it's supposed to be fought, but doesn't have a clue as to what happens when things break down. That additional knowledge may end up being the key."

"Now that's just not true," said Jackson. "We've provided all the essential information. He knows where the changes are gong to be made. Hell, Maddie, we've told him to be on Big Round Top to stop the Rebel advance on it. That's all he needs to know."

She shook her head and started to run a hand through her hair, but the pins holding it up, off her neck, snared her fingers. She dropped her hand to her lap self-consciously and said,"But what happens if there is another change. This isn't a one-shot deal. Brown and his people try to alter the time line back to its proper path and then someone else makes another change. He's an amateur in this."

"Then what about Tucker's assistants. You can't call them amateurs," said Jackson. "Besides that's why we sent them all. They aren't amateurs."

"Who the hell says so?" she snapped. "They've made one trip by accident. They had no idea what was happening when they ended up at the Alamo."

"They, meaning all of them, handled that quite well."

"But that wasn't because they knew what was happening," said Maddie. "They were the only ones time traveling at that point and they knew what they had to do there. Now we've got intervention by another force. I'm in a better position to deal with that."

Jackson twisted in his chair so that he could prop his feet on the bookcase near his desk. He stared at his shoes as if considering everything. Finally he said, "You know that this isn't just a case of us trying to put history back on e right path. There are other factors involved. If the Nazis find out what we're doing, they're going to try to stop it."

She shrugged. "Doesn't matter because the wheels are already in motion. They don't have the capability to time travel. Neither does the United States. It's something that we can do."

"I don't know about that," said Jackson. "Just because we have seen no evidence of their time traveling, it doesn't mean that they aren't. It's in their own self-interest to see this time line preserved. Not to mention that someone is out there. The change proves that."

"Are you suggesting that Nazi scientists have discovered time travel and that they were the ones that changed the outcome of Gettysburg, so that they would win World War Two?"

"Farfetched, I know. But now that the history of the world is as it is, they would want to keep it the way it is. In the world we want, their empire was smashed by the Allies in 1945."

"And in the world we want to create," said Maddie slowly, "our project would not exist. There would be no need for it. No reason for it."

"I'm not convinced that we will eliminate our existence. This project is a natural outgrowth of Tucker's research."

Maddie shook off the dark thoughts that were swirling through her mind. She realized that the course they had elected would change her life significantly. That couldn't be helped. She knew that she would exist in the other world, but had no idea what she would be. It was one of the reasons that she wanted to go to Gettysburg. When the change was made, she would not be affected by it because she would be one of the instruments of it. She would be safe from it.

To Jackson, she said, "But we must have someone there as an observer. Someone who can correlate that history to the right one, and have a knowledge that will allow us, here, to realize our success. It is imperative that we have a representative there, just in case something goes wrong."

Jackson scrubbed his face with his hands. He dropped them to his sides and then leaned his head against the backrest of his chair. Staring at the ceiling, he asked, "Why do you insist on this?"

They had reached the moment of truth. The time had come to forget about science and research and historical perspectives. She leaned forward so that her chin was almost on the edge of the desk and when Jackson looked at her, she said, quietly, "Because Andrew Kent is with them."

Ten minutes later Maddie found herself in the transfer chamber holding onto an Enfield 1855 rifle, a Colt revolver stuck in her belt, waiting for the technicians upstairs to initiate the sequence that would start her trip. She sat on the floor, waiting and watching. A face appeared at the glass and a hand waved at her. She waved back and climbed to her feet.

At that moment, the glow wrapped itself around her and she felt the nausea roll over her. She was dizzy and fell to one knee, steadying herself with the rifle. She looked up as the retrieval bowl disappeared and she began the fall into the past, night and day flashing at her in a quick rhythm like the beating of a wing. She grinned as she felt the waves of hot and cold hitting her as she flashed through the seasons. She saw snow cover the ground in a white blanket that faded quickly. She watched the fields turn green and grow luxurious in seconds, then fade to brown and blow away. She watched it all through half-closed eyes, thinking that she should shut them all the way, but like always, too fascinated by the kaleidoscoping colors and shapes around her.

Then, suddenly, it was bright daylight with a humid heat that engulfed like wet towels in a sauna. She was kneeling on a grassy plain, alone except for the distant sounds of firing. Rifles and muskets and pistols. She opened her eyes wide, searching the broken ground in front of her, wondering what time of day it was. Wondering what day it was.

She got to her feet and began to walk toward the south, keeping the town she could see to her right. She was sure that it was Gettysburg. The limited skyline looked as it did in the pictures she and Jackson had collected and studied before starting the mission.

Then she stopped, looking at the broken ground that lead from her location up to Culp's Hill. Far in front of her she thought that she could see some people moving. A small group, dressed in the dark blue coats of the Union army. She began moving toward them, walking as fast as the broken ground allowed her to.

They didn't see her moving up on them. She watched as they stopped to rest once, and she increased her pace so that she was closer. When they stood, and it looked as if they were starting again, she called out. "Hey! Wait for me!"

Brown turned, but the man in front of him just halted, his eyes straight ahead as if looking for an ambush. Then, as if a command had been given, the men and women around him scattered, taking up firing positions in a rough circle, like they expected to be surrounded at any moment.

It took only a moment for Maddie to catch them. She trotted over the open field and up the slight slope, leaping over the narrow ravines and trenches that split the surface. She ran until she was close to them and then slowed to a walk, her breathing an audible rasp in her throat. She passed the outer edge of the circle, between two of the men who had come in with the last group at the Alamo, and then was in front of Brown.

"What do you want?" he asked her.

She set the butt of her rifle on the ground and leaned on the barrel, breathing hard. There was sweat running down the sides of her face and dripping into the high collar of her blue uniform.

Brown waited a moment and then asked again, "What do you want?"

Still leaning on the rifle barrel, she said, "To go with you and your people. To make sure that everything proceeds as it is supposed to."

"Yeah," said Brown. "Just thought of that did you?"

"Took a while to convince Jackson of the need," she responded. She looked around, spotted Kent and then let her eyes slide away before he had a chance to look at her.

"Is there anything happening that I need to know about," asked Brown.

"Nothing yet. What are your plans?"

"We're going to stake out Big Round Top and wait for the Confederate advance. Once it begins, we send out a scout to warn the Union and try to hold until they do something." He nodded toward Kent. "Andy said that would make the fewest ripples in the fabric of time, if there is a fabric of time to be rippled."

Maddie followed the gaze and stared at Kent who was still watching the ground in front of him. "Yes," she agreed. "That makes the best sense."

"Good," said Brown. He deepened his voice and raised it. "Let's get ready to move out. McGee, you've got the point again."

"Thanks, Colonel."

"You're welcome. Let's move it."

SEVENTEEN

Dennison left Lee's headquarters in the morning feeling better than he had in weeks. The first couple of times he had appeared on the doorstep of the Rebels with information, it was the lower ranking officers who took it, thanked him and sent him packing, as if afraid that he might see something secret. Now, with Meade's Army getting near and Lee without the eyes of his cavalry, they had needed his information. He had been tempted to tell Lee to find Stuart and order the cavalry to return immediately, but Dennison knew that the cavalry would only fight a small skirmish on the third day of the battle and that it would mean nothing in the final outcome.

As he swung himself up into the saddle, he patted his jacket pocket where Lee's letter now rested. After receiving the intelligence from him, Lee had asked if there was anything he could do for him. Dennison had said that a letter telling the Southerners that he was to be trusted would be of great help when he was trying to penetrate the Rebel lines. Lee had smiled at the request and Dennison knew that Lee had realized that such a letter would do little for him in the long run, and if the Union found it, Dennison would probably be shot immediately. Still, Lee moved to a small writing desk, took a single sheet from a drawer and dipped a quill into a small bottle of ink.

"This is the best I can do for you," said the General. "Just a brief letter of introduction."

Dennison took it, scanned it and said, "Thank you, General. This will do nicely."

"Where do you go now, Mr. Harrison?" asked Lee.

Dennison shrugged and then said, "East. Toward Gettysburg. I want to see what happens there."

"Good luck, Mr. Harrison," said Lee. "God go with you and I look forward to seeing you again."

"Thank you, General," said Dennison. He had left and found his way to the road to Gettysburg. Now, a couple of hours later, with the sun climbing into the sky bringing high temperatures, Dennison found himself on the Chambersburg Pike, near the Willoughby Run, with General Henry Heth's Division. Two hours earlier, the advance elements of James Pettigrew's brigade had run into skirmishers from one of Union General Buford's units.

There was sporadic shooting in the distance. Dennison climbed off his horse and lead it forward, glancing right and left, looking for Rebel soldiers. In the back of his mind, he heard the soundtrack of a movie, Errol Flynn playing George Custer saying, "Ride to the sound of the guns."

But the other side of that coin was not to go running into a fight too quickly. It was a good way to get killed. So Dennison walked his horse along the road, searching the terrain for a Rebel unit he could join for a few hours until he was up to the Confederate lines and had a chance to check out the situation.

And then he remembered something that had eluded him during all his attempts to write a history of the War Between the States. Sometime early in the battle, a Rebel general would "capture" the low ground and by noon on the first day, his entire regiment would be prisoners of the Union. The last thing he needed was to be captured along with them. He would have to be careful. If he could find the Rebel commander, maybe he could warn him about his fate.

In front of him, now, he could see billows of blue smoke from the gunpowder drifting upward and to the east. The firing was tapering, then building and tapering again. He tied the reins of his horse to a tree near the side of the road, and using the cover—bushes, tall grass, depressions in the ground—he worked his way forward until he was at the top of a small rise. The land in front of him was spread like the blanket for a picnic. He could see the Rebel units maneuvering.

Gettysburg was three or four miles away. Between it and him was another slight ridge where the Union forces had been scattered and were holding their own. To the south of them, Union cavalry had deployed along McPherson's Ridge. Dennison could see the clouds of smoke boiling out of the trees as the men fired into the Rebel lines.

In front of them, in the woods that bordered a stream, Heth's Division was strung out, returning the Union fire. The open ground between the two forces was obscured by the blue haze of gunpowder drifting to the east.

Dennison crawled to his horse and climbed into the saddle. He turned from the road and headed cross-country, ending up in the trees with Heth's division. There were sentries posted back there, NCO's and lieutenants, watching to make sure that the privates didn't try to run from the battle and to make sure that Union troops couldn't sneak up behind them.

One of the men, a bayonet-tipped rifle in his hand, stepped from behind a tree and yelled, "Halt."

Dennison reined in his horse and sat there looking down at the man. A young man, the new chevrons of a sergeant sown to his sleeve. He waited.

"What ya'all want?"

Dennison was tempted to pull out the letter and see how well it worked, but instead said, "I'm a scout for General Longstreet and have come to look things over."

The soldier stood his ground, studying Dennison carefully and then decided that it couldn't hurt to let him pass. There was only the one of him and several thousand soldiers hidden in the trees. He stepped to the right and waved Dennison on.

Dennison dug his heels lightly into the ribs of his horse and it began to move again, slowly. Around them was the rumble of musket and rifle fire and the occasional boom of an artillery piece. With each crash, the horse jerked, as if surprised and seemed on the brink of bolting. Dennison leaned forward so that his lips were near the animal's ears, patting its neck, he whispered to it, trying to soothe it.

There was another, louder crash, as if a cannon no more than fifty or sixty yards away had fired. The horse reared up, snorting its fear. Dennison tried to clamp his knees together so that he was holding tightly to the horse. He jerked at the reins and the animal stopped kicking. When it was quiet, Dennison slipped from the saddle and tied the reins to a strong tree branch. He could see the horse's eyes rolling wildly with fear as it snorted and shook.

That done, he began working his way through the trees, a light forest with moderate undergrowth. There were bushes clogging the pathways, some vines with stickers on them, and a wet carpeting of leaves. Dennison pushed his way past the small bushes and tiny trees, until he came to a place where everything was trampled down as if a large number of men had been through recently.

Around him he could hear the sound of musket fire. He could hear men shouting at one another, cursing everything from the heat of the morning, to the clouds of smoke that drifted between them and the Union soldiers who were shooting at them.

For a moment he stood watching a soldier fire his weapon and then jerk the ramrod from under the barrel. He jammed it into the end of the weapon, cleaned the barrel and then grabbed the ramrod in his left hand, holding on to the rifle. He dug at the pouch at his belt, took the paper-wrapped cartridge out, bit at the end of it and then pushed it into the barrel. He forced it down with the ramrod, returned that to its place under the barrel and then searched another pouch for the percussion cap. The soldier then crawled forward to a depression near a large tree, aimed and fired. He then retreated, stood, and began reloading.

Dennison watched him go through the process again and fire again. The soldier seemed to have gotten into a rhythm and was paying no attention to what was happening around him. He was like a machine whose function was to load and fire his weapon. He didn't notice the return fire, the bullets tearing through the trees over his head or next to him. He didn't notice the smoke billowing around him. He didn't hear the cries of the wounded or the roar of the artillery. He stood behind his tree, loading his weapon quickly, and then creeping back to the firing line.

Dennison pulled his pistol out and crouched, listening to the shooting as the tempo increased again. It sounded like the Union lines were being reinforced, and Dennison remembered that as being correct. The first skirmishes were with small Yankee units that were slowly reinforced as the morning wore on. Not that it made that much difference because the Rebels still outnumbered them at that point.

On his hands and knees, Dennison worked his way forward, beyond the tree where the soldier was reloading again, to a small depression in the tall grass where he could look out on the expanse of broken ground that rose gently toward the ridge where the Union lines were deployed. Dennison waited. He knew that there would be an attack by a Yankee regiment wearing black hats that would be mistaken for the Army of the Potomac and from that moment, the battle would begin for real.

He jammed his pistol back into his belt and pulled out the binoculars that he had purchased a decade before. A fine pair made in Germany with hand-ground lenses aligned precisely. They were better than most he had seen in the modern world and brought the distant scenes to him as if he was only twenty-five or thirty yards from the action.

From his left came a shout. A man, standing among the trees and bushes pointed and yelled, "Thar comes the black hats! 'Taint no militia! 'Tis the Army of the Potomac!"

Others took up the shout like a battle cry and they began an unplanned advance, out of the trees and onto the open ground. There was volley and fire from both sides. Clouds of heavy blue smoke billowing into existence in flashes of boiling yellow-orange fire to hang over the battlefield.

From the Union lines came a cry and the men in the black hats began a surging charge down the slope, some of them pausing to fire, others just shouting and waving their weapons like banners. They swept into the woods, forcing the Confederate troops to fall back. There was some hand-to-hand fighting, bayonet against bayonet. The clank of metal against metal or against the solid wood of the rifle butts and musket stocks.

Dennison was on his feet, retreating slowly, watching the men in front of him. He saw a Union soldier stagger, tripping over something unseen in the grass as a Rebel jumped him. The bayonet flashed and bright blood bubbled from the man's throat, staining his blue jacket. He dropped his weapon, clawing at his neck as if trying to force air into the wound. He collapsed, tried to stand and then died.

The Confederate stood over the man, like a hunter guarding his prey. There was a look of shocked dismay on his face. He held his weapon with the blood-smeared bayonet pointing at the fallen man. He looked around wildly as if he no longer knew where he was.

A Union officer ran at the Confederate, his sword held high as if he planned to chop the enemy's head from his shoulders. Dennison pulled his pistol and aimed, standing with his right side toward the running officer. As he put his left hand on his hip, taking the classic pose of a duelist, he thumbed back the hammer of his massive Colt. He brought the weapon down slowly until his right arm was completely extended, the pistol held in one hand. As the vertical front sight dropped into the "V" of the rear, and the barrel of the Colt was covering the officer's chest, Dennison slowly squeezed the trigger, waiting for the weapon to fire itself. There was a sudden bang and the pistol bucked in his hand, spewing a cloud of light blue smoke. Dennison was aware of the stink of the burned gunpowder.

The running officer was hit in the shoulder. He lost the grip on his sword and it flipped back over his head to stick into the ground like a penknife thrown by a giant. The man spun, one hand stabbing up to touch his wound as he fell, rolling to his stomach. He started to get to his knees and then dropped forward, as if realizing that he was asking to be shot again.

Dennison hadn't saved the Confederate soldier however. An instant later he was hit in the head by a rifle ball. One second he was watching the fallen Yankee soldier and the next he was spraying blood from the top of his head as he tumbled to his back, his feet and legs jerking spasmodically.

Dennison turned and ran back into the trees, sliding to a halt near a group of soldiers who were waiting for more Union targets. They stood, knelt, or laid in the cover around them. Trees, bushes, depressions in the ground, boulders and tiny mounts of rock and stone they had pushed together with their bare hands as they waited. Some of the obstacles didn't look sturdy enough to turn a rifle bullet, but the men seemed content just to have something in front of them.

Again Dennison jammed his pistol into his belt and grabbed his binoculars. As he raised them to his eyes, he realized that he had made his first real change to history. The other things, telling Longstreet and Lee where the Union forces were, was nothing more than confirming what they had received from other sources. But shooting the Union officer was something different. It was something that hadn't happened in the first battle because Dennison hadn't been there to shoot the man.

And then he didn't care. If he hadn't shot the man, someone else would have. He was too close to the Rebel lines and too obviously an officer to have gotten away unhurt. Dennison might have shot him only a minute before someone else would have. And his act hadn't saved the Rebel soldier either, because he was gunned down within seconds of the Union officer. No, he hadn't made any significant changes yet. But he would.

Through the binoculars he saw a Union officer on horseback, riding among the trees yelling to his troops. Over the noise of the battle, Dennison couldn't hear the words. He lost sight of the man once as the smoke blew across the front, but then a gap opened and Dennison saw the officer again.

At that moment, the man was struck in the head by a rifle shot. There was a crimson splash as the bullet blew out of his head. His right arm flew up almost as if he was calling his men to a halt, his hat spinning away behind him. His horse reared and the man toppled to the ground, a dozen soldiers rushing toward him.

And then Dennison remembered that the senior Union commander on the scene in the beginning of the battle was killed early. The officer just shot had to be General Reynolds who died about ten-thirty or ten-forty on the first morning at Gettysburg.

From behind where Reynolds lay, there was a rising shout and a new Union brigade entered the fight, charging into the Rebel lines. The Confederate forces withdrew then, heading up the slope to Herr Ridge where they stopped.

Dennison turned and ran through the woods, finding his horse where he had left it. He was mildly surprised that it was still there, figuring one of the Rebel soldiers would have stolen it for his escape. He climbed on and galloped toward the Chambersburg Pike, hoping that he could make contact with one of the Rebel colonels who would be leading the men into the railroad gap. He wanted to stop them before they were attacked by the Union brigades maneuvering in that area, but felt he had spent too much time watching the battle from the woods south of the road.

Not that it mattered, because he didn't have any real plans for anything until the next day. July 2 was the day when he would make his influence felt. That was the day he would make the changes that would undercut the Union victory and allow the South to win, not only that battle but also the War Between the States.

EIGHTEEN

David Jackson sat in his tiny office flipping through a history book about the Civil War wondering if his travelers had initiated the changes yet and realizing that they had to have been made. But then he held both of the history books and there was nothing in them to indicate that any changes had been made in the past other than those already accomplished. Things were just as they had been.

This didn't make sense to Jackson because he was nearly two hundred years in the future so that everything should have been changed by now. He thought about that and figured that there must be some kind of "real time" consideration. It was only a couple of hours ago that they had sent the people into the past and if they were retrieved at this precise moment, they would not have had the chance to make their changes.

"Okay," said Jackson out loud, scratching at his ear as his mind ran through it again. The mercenaries had not made the changes yet because they had just arrived in the past. They were now living in "real time," which meant it would be a couple of days in his own time before the changes manifested themselves. He was sure there was a flaw in his thinking somewhere but he couldn't find it. All he knew was that he still had two versions of the battle and that wasn't right. Maybe some changes had been made, but he wouldn't know about them yet. All he could do was sit back and wait for seventy-two hours to pass and then read his books again. He might not realize a change had been made, or wouldn't recognize the exact change if he could spot it, but he was sure that it would be there.

These thoughts began to bother him. It was like watching a spiral spinning. It seemed to draw you in, confusing the input circuits of the mind. Drawing the eyes in and making the stomach flip over. Confusing the mind and body. Making you feel sick like the rocking of a boat, even while the floor was solid under foot.

He got up, walked around his desk, picking at the computer printouts, the felt tip pens, and the history books stacked there. He grabbed one of his coffee cups but there was only a dark smudge at the bottom. He made a face at it and put it down.

So, there was a real time factor in time travel. The mere appearance of the travelers in the past wasn't sufficient to make the change. If that had been true, merely planning the mission might have been enough to activate the change. Once the capability for time travel was invented, then the capability for change was also invented. It meant that they could go do it, and that was the key.

Jackson sat down again, picked up the cup and tossed it up, catching it. That was it. Real time in the past. If the event took three days, then the changes wouldn't manifest themselves for three days.

"Yeah," said Jackson. "Yeah. That's it." He wouldn't know that the change had been made for a couple of days. After the people in the past had time to make it.

He was satisfied with that answer. He reached over to snap off the desk lamp and stood up. As he moved toward the door, there was a rapid hammering upstairs. A muted noise that sounded like someone pounding on a drum in the distance. He reached for the door knob and then dropped his hand, listening carefully.

There was a shout and then a cry of pain. Someone screamed and Jackson retreated into his office. He stood with his back to his desk, staring at the door as if that would provide some clue about the nature of the disturbance outside his office.

Now that he was listening carefully, he heard the whine of the elevator at the end of the corridor, something that he rarely heard. There was the sound of boots on the tile of the hallway floor. Then there was a barked command. Some kind of an order.

Again there was the hammering and this time Jackson recognized it for what it was. A submachine gun firing on full automatic. There was another cry of pain and a thud, as if someone had slammed into the wall.

A moment later, something smashed into the door and it flew open, banging against the wall. Framed there stood a single man, dressed in black, the silver lightning flashes on the collar, the death's head insignia on the peaked cap, and hobnail boots. Jackson stared at the boots, thinking, irrationally, that hobnailed boots belonged in the Twentieth Century. They had no place in this time.

The man held a stubby black weapon, the magazine extending out the bottom. He pointed it in the direction of Jackson. "Who are you?"

Jackson looked around wildly, as if searching for a way

to escape. He turned his attention to the man in front of him and said, "I'm Jackson."

"Then you come with me."

Jackson didn't move. His right hand dropped so that it was resting on the second American history book. His fingers brushed the coffee cup and he wondered if he could hit the man in the face with it. Then he remembered something he had read in a book about the Vietnam War. Never go up against an armed man if you happen to be unarmed.

Jackson stepped forward and asked, "Go where?"

"Up the stairs," said the man. "We will try to stop this experiment before it gets out of hand."

"Upstairs?" said Jackson, glancing at the chronometer set in one of his bookcases. The travelers had been gone for only a few hours. Jackson's mind raced. He wasn't a brave man, and he wasn't a stupid one. All he knew was that he couldn't cave in completely and quickly to this man's orders. He had to do something to delay the Nazis until the change could take affect. Delay was the name of the game with a real goal. If he could delay the Nazis with the appearance of cooperation, then he would win by default. The travelers were somewhere in the morning of the first day and that meant it would be twenty-four hours, at the least, before the change would be made.

"You hurry," said the man gesturing with the barrel of the weapon. "You hurry or I shoot you."

Jackson raised his hands and responded, "Yes. Of course. I'll hurry, but please don't shoot."

Cooperation. That was the name of the game, until sometime in the afternoon tomorrow. All he had to do was delay, and he was sure that he was brave enough to do that.

NINETEEN

Brown led his people south from Gettysburg to the high ground that was west of Culp's Hill, along the Baltimore Pike. They stopped there, flopping down among the boulders and the tall grass, listening to the increasing firing to the west. With his binoculars, Brown could see the Union troops climbing Seminary Ridge. That was the high ground that began west of Gettysburg and swung to the southwest, almost paralleling the Emmitsburg Road where they would form skirmish lines. The fighting would take place there for a great part of the first day.

He could hear the firing on the other side of the ridge and could even see some of the cannons there, but the real battle was going on in the valley on the other side of McPherson's Ridge. The battle wouldn't begin on Seminary Ridge for another few hours.

Brown looked at the people with him. All seemed to be hot and sweaty in their Union uniforms. Crossman looked

113

as if he was about to pass out from the heat. His face was pale and his hair hung down in wet strings.

"You going to be all right?" asked Brown.

Crossman grinned weakly and said, "Too many big meals and too little exercise. It'll be a couple of days before I can go humping through the boonies like I used to."

Maddie moved toward Brown and sat down near him. "What's supposed to be happening right now?" she asked.

"Everybody is jockeying for position. Maneuvering around, trying to find the best positions and waiting for the rest of the army to arrive. Confederates are going to get Seminary Ridge in a little while." He stopped and smiled. "And the Union is going to capture an entire regiment."

"Yeah," she said, interested. "Where's that happen?"

Brown looked at the ground around him, at the town and pointed. "Over there a few miles. There's a railroad cut and a couple of the Rebel regiments get pushed into it. Yankees on both sides pour a murderous fire down into it and the Rebels finally surrender."

"Can we get over there to see it," she asked.

"Why?" said Brown. "We're on foot and still have a ways to go here."

"But we could go see it," she said.

"Yes, I suppose so," said Brown, suddenly angry. It was just the kind of thing people always wanted to see. The blood and gore of traffic accidents. Or the bodies of murder victims. It was the reason they came to fires and went to auto races. To see someone else die. A disgusting desire that kept the newspapers and news programs on the air because their cameramen stuck their lenses in close to photograph the blood.

Brown shook himself and stared at her eager eyes. He remembered seeing woodcuts from the Civil War showing people sitting on the roofs of houses, watching the battles near them. He had heard that the residents of Washington, D.C., had taken picnic baskets to watch the first Battle of Bull Run. Gone out to watch the Army of the Potomac smash the Rebels into a bloody pulp. Watch a few of them die horribly, with blood and entrails thrown around. A great way to spend an afternoon.

He turned away from her and said, "But we're not going over there. No reason for us to go over there. We'll just head for Big Round Top and wait for the battle to shift to us. You'll have all the opportunity to watch all the war you can take."

Then, almost as if to prove that he was correct, a mass of Union soldiers appeared in the distance, moving toward them. Part of the mass broke away, heading west toward Seminary Ridge and then on to McPherson's Ridge. The firing in the distance had died down.

For nearly ten minutes, Brown watched the movement of the troops, fascinated by it. In his own time, in the Vietnam War, he had watched troop movements from helicopters. Small, short lines of men sweeping into treelines or assaulting one end of a village. At the most, he saw two or three hundred men, dressed in green fatigues moving through the verdant jungle. Here were thousands of men, dressed in blue, carrying pennants, guidons and regimental colors. Long lines of men marching toward ridge lines and hilltops. Clouds of dust swirling about them. Officers on horseback riding up and down the columns, shouting orders at the men and urging them on with cries of encouragement.

Brown finally lowered his binoculars and looked at the men and women with him, sitting on the grass, watching the troops. Beyond them, to the north, one of the Yankee columns had split from the main body and was working its way up the gentle slopes toward them.

"Let's get out of here," said Brown. "Move to the south so that we're in position when the fighting resumes."

Without a word, they all got to their feet. McGee took off, trotting about fifty meters to the front to take the point. Once there, he slowed to a walk as the rest of the tiny force fell in behind him.

They worked their way along Cemetery Ridge keeping their eyes on the other ridge lines and the valleys around them. There was sporadic firing from the west as units of both armies stumbled across one another. Brown would have them halt and then search the area near them, but they were too far from the fighting to see anything of importance. They could hear it easily.

They came to the edge of Cemetery Ridge, descending into a saddle, and then climbed up the rough, broken ground of Little Round Top. There were trees scattered over the slopes, bushes spotted around, and boulders pushing up through the ground. There was plenty of cover for the defending forces.

Brown stood at the summit and looked at the western slope where the main Rebel assault would come from. He could see how his tiny force, armed with repeating rifles and even a couple of automatic weapons, should be deployed. How they could stop, at least temporarily, the Rebel attack until more Union soldiers could arrive. He grinned as he realized that he could probably hold the hilltop with only the tiny force with him.

To the south was Big Round Top, the highest ground. It would anchor the Union flank during the last days of the fighting. Brown felt uneasy about leaving it unoccupied, but he knew that the decisive fight would take place where he now stood. Union forces would grab Big Round Top late on the second day, after they had secured Little Round Top. Then, they could watch the fighting in the Devil's

Den and the Peach Orchard. He remembered a description he had read about the Peach Orchard. After the battle it would be possible to cross it by stepping on the bodies of the dead and at no point would his feet touch the ground.

"All right," said Brown. "We've got about a twenty-four-hour wait. Let's settle down and grab a bite."

As the time travelers scattered across the summit of Little Round Top, Maddie moved cautiously to the rear where Andy Kent sat on a rock, his rifle gripped in both hands. She sat on the ground, almost at his feet and said, "I didn't expect it to be so hot."

Kent took out his canteen, a flat, metallic vessel that held almost a quart of water, and drank slowly. He blinked at Maddie, trying to study her without her knowing that he was looking at her.

She wiped a hand across her forehead and then rubbed the perspiration on the front of her jacket. She unbuttoned it so that the light blue, checked shirt she wore under it was visible. She unfastened the collar and then the top and blew down the front as if to cool herself. Then she looked up, saw Kent watching her and smiled slyly.

"Real hot," she said.

Kent capped his canteen and made a production out of putting it away. He wanted to say something to her, but the words stuck in his throat as if he hadn't just taken a drink.

She moved closer and asked, "What's the world like in your time?"

Now he looked at her. He could see the sweat beading on her upper lip, giving her an almost invisible moustache. He tried to keep his eyes on her face, but they strayed lower where he could barely see the curve of her breasts in the opening of her shirt.

"My time," he said. "How do you describe something

like that? A good time? Except that there were always wars going on somewhere and there were people who wanted to dominate other people. Power struggles that resulted in the deaths of thousands. Terrorism and kidnappings." He shook his head, unable to think of a quick way to answer the question.

"Did you like living there?"

He hesitated and then said, "I was going to tell you that it wasn't a fair question because no one could pick the time they lived but I guess we've shot that idea full of holes. But, yes, I suppose I did, if only because of the work we were doing."

She moved closer to him and said, "My time isn't so great now." She turned, staring out toward the west and Seminary Ridge. "Not with the way things are, but we're about to correct that."

"Uh huh," said Kent. He pulled at the grass near him, only half-listening to her words. He was more interested in looking at her, and wondered what she was thinking about him. It seemed that she found excuses to get close to him, but he wrote that off to his own wishful thinking.

"We're harassed by the outside. Foreign governments trying to take everything we have," she said. She moved closer still so that her thigh was lightly resting against Kent's leg as they sat on the grass. "A very bad time for everyone in the world."

Suddenly the red flags went up. The words that had passed him without registering returned, echoing through his head. Her time wasn't so great but they were about to correct that. Maybe there was something more to this than he thought.

He glanced toward Brown who was standing on the western edge of Little Round Top, using his binoculars to scan the ridges to the west. The rest of the mercenaries were sitting on the grass or boulders, paying little attention to anything around them.

He turned his attention back to Maddie, studying her openly. She was a good-looking woman. Intelligent. She had a way with words and avoiding the questions that she didn't want to answer. Kent remembered that no one, during the time they had been in the future, or with any of these people, had volunteered information and each time he had asked, the conversation had been gently turned.

Again he began to suspect that something was going on that he wasn't privy to. Some secret mission that was being engineered by someone else who believed that Kent and his friends were too naive to pick it up.

Of course, they had been taken to the future long after Tuck would have died. Taken into the far future, possibly, but shown nothing of it. He had seen nothing to indicate a technology that was far advanced of that in his own day. Sure, they had refined the hologram techniques, but he knew of a short film, a minute or two, that had been produced in the three dimensions of the hologram in his own time. Hell, he had a friend who had a camera that took 3-D pictures.

Maddie had fallen silent, staring into the distance as if to absorb the sunlight and the bright colors. Her hand had drifted ever so casually over so that it rested on his knee.

He was about to say something when there was a sudden burst of firing in the distance. A crashing of small arms punctuated by cannon shot. The noise grew to a roar.

TWENTY

Dennison had been too slow to stop 42nd Mississippi and the 55th North Carolina. They, along with the 2nd Mississippi, assaulted the Union positions, found themselves in a railroad cut, surrounded and in a devastating crossfire. There was nothing they could do. The majority of the Rebels surrendered then, including all of the 2nd Mississippi.

Now that the fighting had tapered off, Dennison rode to the east along Chambersburg Pike toward the town of Gettysburg. Then he turned to the left, riding north behind the Confederates and climbing Oak Hill where General Rodes had concentrated most of his division. He halted at the front of the Confederate Lines. Heth's division, which had been strung out south of Chambersburg Pike had been badly mauled and had pulled back, but there were other units that had moved into the breech. Other units came from the north so that the Rebels formed a half-moon north of Gettysburg, facing the Yankee soldiers who were guarding the town. Dennison dismounted near a group of Rebels from Rodes Division and watched the show in front of him.

The attack began in mid-afternoon when Rebel General Ewell's II Corps launched an assault. Rodes and his men became a sweeping attack on the Union front. Dennison stood in the background watching thousands of men surge from the cover of the trees, the sunlight flashing on their bayonets as they hit the Yankees. It was a coordinated assault that forced a gap in the Union lines along the Chambersburg Road.

Like the Indian chiefs who sat on horses in the hills and watched their braves attack, Dennison watched the battle unfold, looking for something that he had forgotten during the years in Atlanta as he created his history of the War Between the States, looking for a way to improve the Confederate assault.

The attack surged and ebbed, like the tide on a beach. There were instances where the two sides became mixed with one another and the fighting degenerated into individual battles between the men. Using his binoculars, Dennison was able to watch some of the death struggles as if they had been filmed and were being projected onto a large screen for his amusement.

A group of five Confederate soldiers ran at two of the Yankees. One of the men, kneeling, aimed his weapon and fired, a tongue of flame stabbing out and a cloud of smoke billowing. One of the Rebels dropped his rifle and his hands clawed at the front of his uniform. He took another stumbling step and fell to the ground, his chest a crimson mess.

The second Yankee fired, but missed and then the Rebels were on them. One of the Union soldiers went down quickly, a Confederate bayonet in his belly. But the other soldier was tougher. He had two of them at bay, swinging his rifle back and forth to cover them as he slowly retreated. As one of them danced in close, the man hit him on the head with his rifle barrel. That man dropped but another leaped forward. The Yankee, feinted, parried and thrust. His bayonet penetrated the Rebel's stomach and as he jerked on the rifle, he lost his balance. He let go of his weapon, took a single, hasty step to the rear, and as he fell, the last of the Rebels bayoneted him.

Dennison turned his attention to the whole battle. The noise from it hit him like a solid wall and rolled over him. Shouting, screaming, firing. Men falling and dying with their guts hanging out as they cried or shrieked or just moaned. Dennison was suddenly aware of all that. He saw men fall, missing arms, or legs, or heads. He was close enough to some to hear the wet slaps as the bullets pierced the flesh. Close enough to hear the dying screams or the dying curses. Close enough to see the dirt fly from the coats as the bullets hit and close enough to pick up the coppery odor of the freshly spilled blood.

Involuntarily, he took a step to the rear, as if to gain distance between the battle and himself. He was all too aware of the sights around him. Men lying in piles in the open ground where they had been cut down by rifle bullets and cannon shot. Pieces of men lying on the ground. A perfect arm except for the ragged end where it had been ripped from a man. A boot that was smoking slightly and that was bleeding, the foot still in it.

And the smell. Not the smell of combat in Vietnam where there had always been the stench of death underlying everything, the stink of rotting vegetation in the jungle. Here there was the acrid odor of gunpowder. Huge clouds of it that hung in the air, obscuring everything around it, making the sides vanish and then reappear as the wind played tricks with it. Units disappearing to spring up minutes later several dozen yards from where they had been.

Dennison stood and listened and watched. Listened to the deaths of hundreds of men. Watched them die in splashes of color, or bursts of flame. Watched them tumble to the ground like rag dolls thrown from the porch by an angry child. Hundreds of them sprawled on the ground marking not only their deaths, but the destruction of their units.

Suddenly, out of nowhere, it seemed, came a regiment of nearly fifteen hundred men, their lines straight so that it looked as if they were on parade. They swept out of a copse of trees, a scraggily patch of woods, and entered an open valley, attacking the faltering Yankees. The firing increased. Rifle, musket and cannon, blowing holes in the fine, straight lines of the Rebel soldiers. In a matter of seconds nearly five hundred of those attackers were slammed to the ground, and the assault began to waver.

At that moment a cheer rang out from the Yankee lines. A wild burst of yelling that floated above the sound of the cannons and the crescendo from the muskets. A blue line leaped from hiding and swarmed down on the Rebels firing as fast as they could. In minutes the Rebels were forced to retire, giving up more dead and more prisoners.

For a moment, the fight north of Gettysburg was swinging to the Union side. Dennison watched all this from his position, watched the desperation with which the Rebel commanders scrambled to reinforce their lines and keep the pressure up on the Yankees. There were assaults from both sides. Confederates trying to dislodge the Yankees and the Union counterattacking so that they could hold on for a few minutes more.

Dole, commanding a brigade of men from Georgia had

shifted his troops and was still attacking, but the situation was beginning to look grim. The support he had received from Rodes was deteriorating rapidly. His left was collapsing and it looked as if there would be more losses for the Rebels.

But then Jubal Early's division was in position, concealed by some thick woods. Early's artillery opened fire, ripping holes in the Union lines. J.B. Gordon's brigade of Georgians attacked across nine hundred yards of open ground, ignoring the rifle and cannon fire. They forded a stream, leaped over ravines, attacking the Union position, dislodging them.

Union officers tried to stem the rout and threw up a makeshift line, but Early tossed in the rest of his division. The Union line shattered and began a retreat. But that retreat degenerated into flight as the Rebels kept up their pressure, their rifles and cannons destroying the Yankee integrity.

Dennison could stand it no more. He had watched too much. He leaped to his horse, dug his heels in and raced down the hill to join the Rebels as they began their assault on the town. To his left, Heth and the Rebels there began a new attack, pushing the Yankees from McPherson's Ridge toward Seminary Ridge.

Dennison joined Abner Perrin's South Carolina Brigade as it slammed into the Yankees, forcing them out of Gettysburg. Dennison entered the town carefully, his eyes on the windows of the buildings, searching for snipers. He realized that he was exposing himself to unnecessary danger by riding in. Exposing himself to a sniper, who would believe that he was an officer. He swung out of the saddle and tethered his horse. Gripping his rifle in both hands, he followed a group of Confederates as they ran down a street, half of them on one side and half on the other.

Firing suddenly erupted, the bullets striking the wood of the buildings and shattering the glass of the windows. Dennison, when a round smashed the window next to him, dived for cover. He rolled once and came up in a doorway, crouching in the shadow. He let his eyes play across the street, searching the second and third stories of the buildings, and then the rooftops, looking for the Yankee sharpshooter.

He saw nothing and was about to step into the open when he realized that he had given the enemy time to reload. He ducked back and again studied the windows. Dennison realized that the man knew what he was doing. He was staying well back from the window so that he couldn't be easily spotted from the outside.

Dennison stuck his head out, into the light and ducked back quickly, trying to draw the enemy fire, but the sniper didn't shoot. Across the street, he saw three men running along the side of a building. They stopped at the corner and one of them fired his weapon at a target that Dennison couldn't see.

There was a rippling of return fire and one of the Rebels fell, his hands around his thigh. He rolled so that he was next to the wood of the building. He lay on his back, holding his leg up so that it nearly touched his chest. He was yelling at the other two men who had fled around a corner, taking cover. Dennison couldn't hear the words, but the tone of the voice suggested the man was more angry than hurt.

At that moment, a shadow flashed by him and another soldier ran along his side of the street. Dennison poked his head out in time to see the muzzle flash of the Yankee weapon as he fired at the running Rebel.

Dennison pushed his own rifle out, aimed at the center of the second-story window, and fired. He kept his eye on it, but nothing happened. It meant that he had either missed, or that the Yankee had fallen back, deep inside where he couldn't be seen.

Without waiting to find out, Dennison left his cover, running up the street until he reached the corner. He stopped there, listening to the firing going on around him. There was the booming of cannon and Dennison ventured a glance around.

In the town square, he saw a battery of artillery, six cannons, firing down the streets. They had been there for a while, since they had had the time to set up, but now it was looking as if they would have to retreat soon. Dennison could see Rebel soldiers piling up in the streets, out of sight of the Union cannoneers, waiting for the opportunity to rush them. Rifle bullets were kicking up the dirt around the Yankees.

Their commander realized that they were about to be overrun. Before the attack could get started, he ordered his men out of the square, following the rest of the Union Army. As they moved, so did the Rebels, swarming out of the streets, yelling their battlecries. In seconds, the main town square was in the hands of the Confederates and the battle had shifted again. Now it was taking place on the south side of Gettysburg where two Union generals were trying to get their men up Cemetery Hill.

Dennison decided that he had had enough of the fighting. He turned and ran back until he found the door to one of the taller buildings. He raced up the stairs to the third floor and then to the windows on the west side. Through the smoke generated by the attack on the town and by small fires started by the fighting, he could see part of Seminary Ridge.

Now the major fighting had shifted there. The Rebels had forced the Union to abandon their positions on McPherson's Ridge, but the Yankee generals had managed to consolidate their position, forming a line on Seminary Ridge. The Union was being pushed back, but fighting stubbornly.

Dennison ran down the stairs and out onto the street, suddenly overcome with a desire to see the battle on Seminary Ridge. He raced through the town, found the place where he thought that he had left his horse, but this time his luck didn't hold. It was gone.

Not that it mattered. There were hundreds of loose horses running around. Dennison moved to the side of the street and when one ran by, he snagged the reins. He jerked the horse's head around and the animal reared on its hind feet, but it settled down quickly.

As Dennison swung up into the saddle, his hand slipped in a patch of wet and when he glanced at his palm, it was red. The former owner of the horse had been shot out of the saddle.

Dennison turned, heading west, staying behind the Rebel lines until he came to the Chambersburg Pike. He crossed the road to the west of Seminary Ridge, angling along McPherson's Ridge, slipping in behind Heth's division which had re-entered the fight.

He came up behind them, the seminary, for which the ridge had been named, rising in front of him. Some of the structures were four stories tall and surrounded by trees. The battle lines had been drawn. Long lines of soldiers, their banners waving in the center of them, firing at each other from almost pointblank range. Behind them the officers rode horses, their swords waving in the air.

For a moment the battle hung stalemated that way. Long lines of men, their rifles leveled and belching fire and smoke. There was shouting and yelling. One of the Union soldiers grabbed an American flag and ran to the front of the Union position with it, waving it back and forth. A second later he was cut down by a Rebel volley. Another man grabbed the flag before it could touch the ground and then retreated with it. He stopped near the center of a column, holding the flag high.

Suddenly, there was a surging charge from the Rebels. They burst from their own lines, their heads down like men fighting a hurricane, forcing their way forward. Some were shouting, some were just trying to cover the ground between the opposing forces before they died. Then they were mixed with the Yankees, bayonet against bayonet, metal clanking against metal, pistols being used. The Rebels smashed through the center of the Union line breaking it in two. Men turned to flee and the Rebels cut them down.

More Rebels were jammed into the break, turning right and left, rolling the flanks away from them. At that point, there was nothing that the Union commanders could do except retreat. They ordered their men back away from Seminary Ridge, falling across the open ground, the Emmitsburg Road and toward Cemetery Ridge where other Union elements were forming.

Dennison watched as some of the Rebels gave chase until ordered to return by their own officers. Then the men swept the field looking for wounded from both sides. Dozens of men had been taken prisoner and were herded to the rear to be guarded by Heth's division until transport to prisoner-of-war camps in the South could be arranged.

But now it was late in the day. Dennison could still hear firing as the two sides tried to break off the engagements, pulling back to regroup. Dennison rode across the battlefield, through the Seminary and stopped at the forward edge of the Confederate lines. He climbed from his horse, held the reins in one hand and dug out his binoculars. He swept the field in front of him, looking up at the Union forces as they worked to establish a defensible position.

Dennison crouched and continued to watch. He knew that the Confederates had won the day. There had been some minor setbacks, like the surrender of an entire regiment, but there had been some big victories too. They had forced the Union out of positions it had held, took the town of Gettysburg from them and had generally beat them on the battlefield. Union casualties were about a third again as heavy as those suffered by the Rebels.

But this, Dennison knew, wasn't the crucial point. Tomorrow would mark the day when the battle could be turned. Dennison glanced to his left, where General Longstreet would be forming his corps. Tomorrow, Dennison would have to appear at Longstreet's headquarters and convince him of the need to take the Round Tops. The Union forces would be strung out along Cemetery Ridge, wrapping around to Culp's Hill and the Rebel strategy would be to attack there. Dennison didn't care about that, as long as Longstreet sent a regiment, or better yet, a brigade, to take and hold the Round Tops. That done, they could harass the Union flanks, forcing them to deploy men on that edge of the battle, weakening their lines. In the long run, it would cause the Union defeat at Gettysburg.

Dennison put his binoculars away and climbed back into the saddle. He rode to the rear of the lines. Already the soldiers had stacked their weapons and were cooking their evening meals. There were sentries out, pickets out, and men were putting up tents, or fighting for space in the buildings of the seminary. He stopped near a circle of men who had built a smoking fire and erected a spit over it.

Two birds, stripped of feathers, were already roasting there, dripping grease.

Dennison hesitated, then leaned closer and asked, "How you boys doin'?"

The oldest of them, a man with gray coloring his otherwise black hair and corporal stripes sown to the sleeves of his uniform, said, "Chickens are ours. We found them." He smiled. "Captured them fair."

"No doubt," said Dennison. "We gonna stomp some Yankee ass tomorrow."

One of the men held up a cup containing a steaming liquid. "Yeah. Kick ass," he shouted happily. "Just like today."

"Eat hearty," said Dennison. "Lots to do tomorrow. Lots of fighting to be done."

He rode off to the rear of the lines and then turned to the south. Tomorrow, he thought to himself. If Longstreet would listen. Or maybe General Hood who would be in an even better position to grab the Round Tops. It didn't matter who it was, just as long as it was done. As long as one of them grabbed the Round Tops.

But that was tomorrow.

TWENTY-ONE

Jackson stepped into the hallway and looked at the body sprawled there. She had been one of the technicians working on correlating the data from the first history with that of the second. Jackson didn't want to stare at her, he wanted to reach down and feel for a pulse. There was a pool of blood under her back and three bullet holes stitched across her chest. She lay with her head and a shoulder up against the wall. Her eyes were partially opened, almost as if she was looking down her nose at the bullet holes in her body.

There was a hand on Jackson's back, pushing toward the elevator at the end of the hall. As he walked along it, he saw other doors had been kicked in. Some of the offices were occupied. Technicians held at gunpoint by men and women in black uniforms. Jackson wanted to tell everyone not to worry because, one way or the other, it would be over shortly. But he didn't dare speak to anyone.

They stopped at the elevator. Jackson stared at the brushed aluminum of the door, seeing the dim, almost recognizable reflections in it. He glanced at the man and asked, "Where are we going?"

The Nazi glared at him and said, "Upstairs. To your transfer chamber."

"Oh? And?"

"And you're going to recall the people that you sent into the past. Get them back here." The Nazi leaned forward and pushed the button on the elevator. "Then we'll decide whether any of you should be shot."

"There is a treaty between us—meaning my government and yours," said Jackson. He was pleased to notice that his voice wasn't trembling. Much.

The man smiled. It was an evil grin showing teeth that looked like they had been filed to points. "I would think that your activities here have negated any agreements that our governments might have entered into. And if that didn't, then our raid on your complex did."

The doors on the elevator opened and the Nazi shoved Jackson in. Jackson hit the rear wall, hesitated and then turned. "I'm afraid that I don't know what you mean."

"Don't lie to me," said the man. "I'm not in the mood. He pushed the button on the elevator that would take them to the ground floor.

The doors shut and there was the sudden sensation of great weight as the elevator accelerated. An instant later that was replaced by weightlessness and then the doors popped open.

As Jackson stepped out, he felt a hand grab his shoulder. "Let's be clear on this, Jackson. We're not joking here. You saw the body in the hallway. If you fuck with us, we'll kill you. That's all there is to it."

In front of him, Jackson could see the corridor. A

brightly lighted corridor, trimmed with stainless steel and tile and light green paint. Nothing on the floor, or rather nothing that was supposed to be on the floor. Jackson could see a smear of blood dripping down one wall and pooling on the floor. The body of a man lay halfway to the other end of the hallway. He was wearing a suit and had dropped a bundle of papers. Jackson didn't know who it was because he was lying face down.

"We hold the whole building and according to our calculations, it will be two to three hours before your army can get here. Another two to three before they will have sufficient force to dislodge us." He grinned his evil grin. "Plenty of time."

They approached one of the doors and the man threw it open. It was the conference/briefing room off to one side of the transfer tank controls. A huge room that could hold all thirty of the technicians, the travelers, the briefers and another fifteen or twenty people. Now all the furniture had been shoved against one wall and there were nearly fifty people sitting on the floor. A dozen men and women, dressed in the black of the SS, stood guard over them.

The man let Jackson enter slowly. Jackson stared at the people, noticing that all had their hands behind their backs. As he stepped into the room he saw a woman whose back was to him. Her hands were lashed behind her with a plastic strip. Another cable tie pulled her elbows cruelly together, giving her a stiff, uncomfortable posture.

The Nazi saw where Jackson was looking and pushed past him. He jerked the woman to her feet. She was slender, with long dark hair hanging to her shoulder blades. She was wearing the standard coverall. The Nazi grabbed the zipper and tugged it down so that it was covering her bellybutton. He reached inside cupping her breasts.

The woman stood still, her eyes closed, trying to ignore what was happening to her.

"You see," said the man. "We have complete power over all of you. Now, you tell us who you need to retrieve those travelers, and nobody will get hurt."

Jackson didn't move. He let his gaze sweep over the room, covering the people in there. Most of them hadn't looked up, afraid that they would call attention to themselves.

The Nazi pulled his hand from the woman's coverall. Without warning, he slammed it into her stomach. She doubled over, fell to her knees and rolled to her side. Her mouth was working as she tried to suck air into her lungs. She was lying in a fetal position and would have wrapped her arms around her stomach if they hadn't been bound behind her.

"I can make it a lot worse for your people," said the man. "I can take five or ten of them out of here and shoot them. I can shoot five or ten of them in here and make you all watch. I can beat them senseless if I so desire." He stopped talking and drew a foot back, as if to kick the woman in the kidney. "You can help me complete my task, or you can be brave with the lives and bodies of your co-workers. But in the end, you'll do as I say."

Jackson looked at the woman on the floor at his feet. Her first name was Sarah and she had spent seven years in college studying for a job here. She was a pretty girl. A quiet one who had a mind like a steel trap. Jackson felt his eyes burning as if he was about to cry because of the pain he had caused her. He blinked rapidly so that the Nazi wouldn't know how upset he was. He turned so that he could see the clock on the wall. Less than twenty-four hours for the change. But twenty-four hours for him to delay without having his people tortured and killed.

"We might have a problem with retrieval," said Jackson, looking at the Nazi. "It's not scheduled for another couple of days and if we move it forward, we might have trouble locating all the subjects."

"I'm not interested in the problems you foresee," responded the man. "I want results."

"Yes, but I'm just warning you that . . ."

"You warn me of nothing. You perform your mission or your people are going to die." He snapped his fingers and pointed at one of the male technicians. A Nazi grabbed the man under the arm, jerking him to his feet. "Take that man out and shoot him as an object lesson."

"No!" screamed the man. "You can't do that. Please! I'll help you. I know what to do. Please!"

"Get him out of here," snapped the leader. "Now!"

The man struggled, jerking his shoulders free of the Nazi soldier's grasp. Another grabbed him, and shoved him toward the door. The man stumbled and fell. A third man opened the door and they kicked the technician out. He shrieked with the pain and once in the corridor, out of Jackson's sight, began screaming. As the door swung closed on its hydraulic hinges, there was a single shot that cut off the screams.

Jackson felt his head swim. He wanted to sit down, but there were no chairs. He sagged and put out an arm to brace himself against the wall. "Please," he said. "That wasn't necessary. We'll cooperate. We're scientists, not soldiers. Just give us a chance. Give us time." But even as he spoke he realized that he was a time traveler himself. If the opportunity presented itself, he could return to the past and fix it so that Davis wasn't draggged out and shot. Or erase the beatings that his people might have to undergo. As long as he could buy enough time. Buy his twenty-four hours.

"You have no time left. You do as ordered." He bent and helped Sarah to her feet. He pulled his dagger from the scabbard. For the most part, it was a ceremonial knife, not meant for combat, but it was extremely sharp. "I know you will help," said the man.

"Please," said Jackson. "You don't have to do any more."

"No," said the man. "I don't think that you believe me." He slipped the knife inside Sarah's coverall and ripped upward, cutting the material from her shoulder. He turned, jammed it in the other side and did the same thing. Then grabbing a handful of material, he cut the right sleeve away. The coverall dropped, revealing her to the waist. There was a darkening bruise just under her breastbone. The man was pleased that she wore neither a blouse nor a bra under her coverall.

He stared at her breasts and touched the tip of the knife into the soft area under her chin, slowly applying pressure. She whimpered as the knife cut her and a drop of blood slid down her neck, stopping in the hollow between her collarbones.

"I know that you don't want any more of your people hurt, but I don't want a lot of shit from you either. You do your job and this lady won't have to suffer anymore. Fuck around with me and I'll fuck around with her."

"Please," said Jackson. "We'll do as you say. Just don't hurt anyone." And as he said it, he realized that he had to do something to delay the Nazis because that was the only way to ensure that they all got away. Even the man they had just murdered.

TWENTY-TWO

Like most of the others, Brown had spent the afternoon at the western edge of Little Round Top watching the battle. He had heard the firing increase in volume until it was a continual roar. He had heard the roar punctuated by cannon blasts and had seen the wavering blue lines as they appeared on Seminary Ridge. As he had watched, the binoculars unable to resolve the distant images, the line stabilized, waiting. There were American flags and regimental flags and flapping pennants. A gray line appeared like an apparition from a heavy mist and the firing had begun again.

Both the lines seemed to burst into fire and smoke. He saw flashes of orange, bright flashes obscured by the swelling clouds of smoke and dust. There had been a clash there. The sound of a hundred thousand thunderstorms as the lines shot at each other. As the cannon boomed and the horses screamed. The surging lines touched near the buildings of the seminary and then disappeared in clouds of smoke as the two sides fought for the ridge.

Behind him, Brown heard one of the women gasp and then Maddie was at his elbow, demanding, "Why are we here? We should be there pushing the Rebels back."

Brown lowered his binoculars and stared into her hazel eyes. Studied her face for a moment and then said, "Our place is here. You told us that. The fight on Seminary Ridge is going just as history demands. A large battle with the Union finally being pushed away."

"But we could help them," she said quietly.

"But we don't want to help them," said Brown. "We have to be here so that we can stop the Rebels when they try to take Little Round Top. Everything else is just as it should be. If we abandon this position and try to change the course of the battle at a different place, we could lose the opportunity to fix it here. No. We stay put."

Maddie looked at him for a minute and then turned so that she was facing the fight on Seminary Ridge. Watching through the haze and dust and smoke as the Union center collapsed and the Rebels forced troops through the gap.

"It's too late now, anyway," she mumbled.

"But the crucial fight will happen tomorrow and we're ready for it."

That had been hours ago, with the sun hanging in the western sky, glowing a blood red as if in mourning for the thousands who had died during the day. Brown had put his binoculars away, and sat with his back to a large rock, facing east. He could hear the firing on scattered parts of the field, but knew that the real fighting had ended for the day. Knew that both sides were licking their wounds, collecting the injured and preparing for the battle the next day.

He watched his tiny force gather wood for a fire to heat the evening meal. He had told them that they would have to put out the fire at dusk because he didn't want anyone, on either side, to see it. That might give some bright boy the idea to secure the ground during the night and that was the last thing that he wanted. He wanted to be left alone until it was time for the fight to begin. Late in the afternoon the next day.

Now it was dark. Had been for a hour or so. The mercenaries had eaten their meal, kicked the fire out, and buried the scraps of food so that the enemy could not find them. The night was overcast and the humidity, along with the smoke of the burnt gunpowder, hung in the air. They didn't have to move to work up a sweat. Each prayed that it would rain and break the heat and each knew that it wouldn't, because it hadn't.

Maddie had watched Brown through most of the afternoon, wondering how he could calmly stand there and watch the battle. She had wanted to run down the slope and join in. Had actually wanted to feel the recoil of her weapon as she pulled the trigger. Had wanted to see the bayonet flashing sunlight as it penetrated an enemy soldier's chest. She didn't recognize the bloodlust that sometimes overwhelmed soldiers at the beginning of a fight and made them commit acts they would never think themselves capable of. She didn't realize that the hate boiling in her was not directed at the subhuman Rebels, but at the men who wanted to smash her way of life. To smash her.

She had begun to shake with the tension. She looked around wildly, her breath coming in short gasps. She shifted her weight from foot to foot and when that wasn't enough, paced in a tight circle, slamming her feet into the ground so that she could feel the vibrations up her legs and in her gut. Her knuckles were white on the barrel and stock of her rifle where she gripped it. She couldn't sit still.

And then she had felt Kent's arm on her shoulder. He hadn't said anything to her, just stood beside her, pressing close, almost holding her. She shot a glance at him and saw that he seemed to be calm, almost relaxed and there was a new excitement in her.

The bloodlust flipped and she felt a desire that was a physical pain. She felt a tightening in her chest and her nipples were rock hard. A warmth spread down her belly and she wanted to turn and kiss him. Wanted to force her tongue into his mouth, crush her hips against his.

Instead, she turned her attention to the others. They stood watching the fight, watching the battle. None seemed to be reacting to it the way she was. She was embarrassed by the flood of emotions washing over her.

With one hand she let go of the rifle and felt herself searching for Kent's hand. She gripped it, squeezing it until Kent looked at her and asked, "Are you all right?"

She turned and threw herself at him, holding him tightly muttering, "No. No, I'm not all right. I don't know what to do." She felt tears in her eyes and didn't understand that either. She twisted slightly so that she could look at the battlefield.

A moment later, Kent was turning her so that she was looking to the south, toward the rise of Big Round Top and the woods there. Now she could no longer see the battlefield. She could hear the fighting, but no longer see it.

"You've got to relax," said Kent, soothingly.

That was a stupid thing for him to say, and then she realized that it didn't matter what he said as long as he kept talking. Kept telling her things until the turmoil of emotions drained from her. Suddenly her knees felt weak, trembling, and she wanted to sit down. She wanted to close her eyes and sleep.

When she awoke, it was dark. Her head was cradled in

Kent's lap, his fingers in her hair. She could feel sweat on the back of her neck and under her arms. At first, she refused to open her eyes because she was suddenly so calm, so at ease.

She opened her eyes slowly but could see no one else near them. She struggled to sit up, her bones aching, her joints stiff. "Where are the others?" she asked.

Kent stood, brushing the dirt and dead leaves from his clothes. "Over there, behind those rocks where they can keep their eyes on the Confederate camps. Longstreet has finally deployed his men as he was supposed to, according to history."

"Did you eat?"

"Wasn't all that hungry," said Kent. He grinned, his teeth white in the night. "Besides, you were in quite a state."

She turned her back on him and looked at the dark expanse of ground dropping away from her. She thought that she could see the Rebel lines on the other side of the Peach Orchard, behind the Devil's Den and along the Emmitsburg Road.

"I don't know what came over me," she said.

"Don't worry about it. It's a common enough reaction during your first big fight. You either run into the middle of it or run away from it."

She turned to face him. "And you know all about that, I suppose, being a scientist yourself."

"I wasn't always a scientist," said Kent. He reached down and picked up a pointed stick. As he drew in the soft dirt, he said, "In my time, some of us couldn't afford to go to college and that meant you either volunteered for the service to get the benefits of the G. I. Bill, or you were drafted. I spent my time in the Army learning the art of shooting holes in my fellow human beings."

She arched an eyebrow, but Kent couldn't see it in the dark. She stepped closer and asked, "Then you've been in war before."

"If you can call Vietnam a war. Yes, I've been in combat before. Nothing on the scale of this." And then he stopped, remembering the Alamo. Thousands of Mexican soldiers storming the wall of the old mission. "And the Alamo," he added. "And the Alamo."

Now she stood next to him, so close that she could feel the heat of his thigh near hers. She groped in the dark, found his fingers and held his hand, wishing that he would do something, make a move.

Then, in the night, they heard a clattering. First just a thin sound a long way away and then something that built. Equipment rattling. Leather creaking. Commands not shouted, but whispered almost. The beat of horses' hooves.

Kent moved away from her, distracted. He walked toward the slope of the hill to the east and looked into the night. Meade and the majority of the Army of the Potomac were coming up Taneytown Road, past the foot of Little Round Top.

When Maddie came up beside him again, he said, "That's got to be Meade. Everything is going just as it's supposed to. Just like history demands."

"Is it?" she asked as if she couldn't believe it. As if the whole thing was a pipe dream.

"We better get back to the others," said Kent. He turned and nearly bumped into her. He put out his hands and felt the softness of her breast. He jumped back and muttered, "Sorry."

"Don't worry about it," she snapped. "I didn't feel a thing."

Together they crossed the rough ground of the Little

Round Top, working their way among the trees and light brush that grew there, and around the boulders and rocks scattered on it. They came up to Brown, who was sitting on one of the rocks, the binoculars to his eyes as he surveyed the ground below him.

"Meade's here," said Kent.

Brown lowered the binoculars and faced them. "Good. Right on time. So far there haven't been any real changes. At least as far as I can tell."

He looked at the two of them, just shadows in the dark and added, "You know, Lee's orders had been to avoid a general engagment here. His subordinates entered into the battle more or less on their own. Lee wanted to force Meade to attack him so that he would have the defensive."

"Doesn't matter now, does it," said Kent. "The battle is joined and it is progressing just as it should." He shot a glance out of the corner of his eyes, wondering if there was more to this. His suspicions of the afternoon had not changed radically. He was still afraid that there was something more going on.

"Until tomorrow," Maddie reminded them.

"Until tomorrow," agreed Brown. "Listen, why don't you two grab some sleep. Kent, I want you to take a stand at guard at three. Two-hour shift."

"Delightful," said Kent.

"What about me?" asked Maddie.

"You'll just get to sleep through the night," said Brown. "I've got everyone else taking a turn though."

"How did I luck out?"

"You're not trained for this sort of thing," said Brown. "The rest are. Simple as that."

As they turned to move toward the center of the hill, Brown called softly. "When did you plan to pull us out of here? After the battle, or after the Union firmly establishes itself on Little Round Top?"

"I haven't thought that much about it," she said. "I was going to watch until I was sure that we had stopped the Rebels." She rubbed a hand over her face and then wiped the sweat on the front of her uniform. "I guess that means that we have to stay until Pickett makes his charge. We make our change tomorrow but have to wait until the next to confirm its success. Besides, we have to make sure that Custer doesn't get killed at Hanover."

"Yeah," said Brown. "That's what I suspected."

"You have a problem with that?" asked Maddie.

"No," said Brown. "It's just that this messing with time bothers me and the longer we're in place in the past, the more chances there are for us to do something that will screw up something else in history."

"But we haven't done anything yet," she said. "We've stayed in the background and watched the battle being fought. We haven't fired a shot."

"And we don't know how fragile time might be, " said Kent. "Our mere presence may affect it, or we might be able to do a lot without history noticing it. Gettysburg is one of those pivotal events where the wrong thing done at the wrong time has devastating consequences in the future."

"That's what I mean," said Brown. Then added quickly, "Though I guess we can't screw it up any more than it's already screwed up."

"There is that," said Maddie. "Talk to you in the morning."

"Right," said Brown. "In the morning."

TWENTY-THREE

Dennison stayed near the seminary for several hours, watching the Union lines until night fell. Then, accepting the offer of a small group of Rebel NCOs, he sat down to eat. The meal was made of food scrounged from the country, thrown into a large black pot to make a stew and then handed out to all who stopped by. It was a gigantic stew and as the evening progressed, more food was tossed in.

Dennison listened to the talk of the men around him, trying to get a feel for them. There was a great deal of laughter and joking. The men felt good. They knew that a large number of their fellows were dead and a greater number were missing, but that didn't change the fact that they had met what was considered the best army the Union had. And they had beaten them.

There was no reason to tell them that the men they thought were members of the Army of the Potomac were really part of a Wisconsin regiment. Dennison had remembered that when he heard the first shouts from the Rebels. He just sat, watching and listening because he knew that the next day, July 2, was the important day.

Finally he got to his feet, thanked the men for their hospitality and shouted, "We'll get them tomorrow."

As he climbed on his horse, there was a cheer behind him. He swung around, rode to the west to put Seminary Ridge between him and the Yankees and then turned south. All around him he could see the campfires of the Confederates. They were shielded from the Union by the high ground of Seminary Ridge. There was a lot of noise in the Rebel camps. Laughing, joking and singing. They were wrestling with each other. Officers stood to the side watching, instinctively knowing that to try to put a stop to it would undermine the emotion of the troops. It could somehow swing the emotion from the Rebels to the Yankees. They wanted the troops to keep the feeling they had. They wanted them to be ready to attack in the morning.

Dennison stopped once, dismounted and walked into a group of soldiers from Heth's division. They were a little more subdued than some of the others, but the high feelings still ran through their camp. They were working on their equipment, cleaning their rifles, sharpening their knives and bayonets, and replenishing their powder. They had been involved in some of the heaviest fighting of the day, and still, they were excited. They had the attitude of winners.

He left without talking to anyone. He was more interested in the feelings, the textures of the battle. He was interested in seeing how the men reacted to a full day's fighting. He suspected that in the coming months, as the men had a chance to reflect on the battle, there would be problems for them. As they moved into civilian life where killing and fighting were frowned on, they would have emotional problems. There would be men who couldn't adjust and they would end up in the army fighting Indians on the plains, or become adventurers in the southwest. Some would become emotional cripples, realizing that they had been happily gunning down fellow humans. Most would adjust completely, seeing their activities in the war as just another part of their lives.

Dennison climbed back into the saddle and rode farther to the south, searching for Longstreet's headquarters. Now that the battle had been joined, it was important that he give Longstreet the last bit of intelligence. Without Stuart and his cavalry to tell Longstreet and Lee where the enemy was, where his strong points were, Dennison would be invaluable in that respect.

He entered a light wood, came to a stream and followed it. He could see Rebel soldiers scattered through the woods, dozens of them around smoking campfires. These men were talking with one another in low tones and the fires were small, hidden behind trees and large rocks so that the Union soldiers on Cemetery Ridge to the east wouldn't see them.

There were sentries. Some of them stopped him, but then let him pass. He didn't have to take out his letter to show them. Finally he broke out of the woods and in the distance saw a farmhouse. He rode toward it, figuring that Longstreet or his staff would be using it as a command post.

There were guards outside it. A dozen of them easily visible around the house and Dennison hoped there were more, hidden in the bushes and in the hedge. There was a low barn fifty yards away and Dennison heard laughter from it. A platoon or more were inside it.

He climbed out of the saddle and walked the horse up to

the short picket fence just a few yards from the house. A corporal stopped him by stepping into the pathway.

"What'd ya'll want?"

"I'm here to see General Longstreet," said Dennison.

"I'm sure ya'all are, but I've instructions ta keep everyone away from the headquarters."

"You're making a mistake, Corporal," said Dennison. "I'm going to put my hand in my coat and give you a letter. I take it you can read."

The corporal didn't say a word. He stood waiting and took the letter when it was handed to him. He studied it intently, moving it around, trying to catch the light from the moon, although it was hidden frequently behind the clouds. After a few minutes, the Corporal said, "I'll have to check with the Sergeant." He handed the letter back and yelled, "Sergeant of the Guard, post number four."

Dennison took his paper and smiled. He had given it to the man upside down and he had never noticed. Not that it mattered since the corporal was calling for the sergeant anyway.

A moment later a huge man loomed out of the dark and demanded, "What in the hell is all the shouting going on over here."

"Man here wants to see the General. Has a paper."

The sergeant held out a beefy hand and said, "Let me see that paper."

"You can read?" asked Dennison.

"Course I can read. Ya'all think I'm a rube?"

Dennison handed the letter over, upside down and watched as the sergeant squinted at it. Then he shot a glance at Dennison and turned it over. "Think ya'all's smart, don'cha?"

He read it, holding it up and moving it around to catch

the light and then said, "Holy mother of God. This here is signed by Gener'l Lee hisself."

"I guess the corporal missed the signature," said Dennison.

"I'm sure he did, sir," said the Sergeant. "If ya'all follow me, I'll see that you get inside."

Dennison reached out and took the paper back, folding it so that he could put it into his pocket. He noticed that the paper was slightly damp from his sweat and hoped that the ink wasn't going to smear. He doubted that he could convince General Lee to give him another. He'd try to find something to carry it in to protect it.

He followed the Sergeant along a dirt path to a wooden porch. There were two men standing guard there. When they saw the sergeant, one of them leaned over and opened the door.

As Dennison stepped in, he noticed that thick blankets had been tacked over the windows. A dozen lamps with their wicks turned high burned brightly so that the room was bathed in light. There was a large map tacked to the wall and half a dozen officers standing around it. Dennison could make out the symbols marking the locations of the Confederate forces and the suspected locations of the Yankees.

One of the men turned when the door was opened, stared at the sergeant and then Dennison and said, "Close the damned door." He glared at the sergeant. "Don't ya'all know better than to come waltzing in here without knocking." He looked significantly at the map.

"Don't worry, Major," said Dennison. He took out the letter again and handed it to the man.

After the major had read it, Dennison said, "I can help you with the distribution of the Yankee soldiers. I know where most of them are."

The Major glanced at the letter again and asked, "Ya'all just rode out there and looked at the Yankees and they let you?"

"No sir. I made way along the lines and took a look at the placement of the pickets and skirmishers. I saw a couple of battle flags this afternoon and putting that together, with a couple of other things I saw, I know how the Yankees are positioning themselves."

"I believe we know that too." The Major hung onto the letter.

Dennison moved to the map and studied it. One of the lieutenants stared at him, wondering if he should say something. Dennison smiled at him and then pointed. "First thing you don't know is that Meade and the bulk of his Army of the Potomac have arrived. Right now he's behind Cemetery Ridge, but by morning he'll have his troops scattered all along it."

The Major nodded. "Yeah. We figured that he would be coming up but didn't expect him quite yet."

"The Yankees are consolidating their positions all along the ridge, concentrating their forces to the north, on Cemetery Hill and Culp's Hill. But I think, given the placement of the pickets and skirmishers, one of those divisions or Corps, is going to move off the ridge tomorrow, entering the Peach Orchard. They'll kind of bow the line out and leave their flanks exposed."

"Meaning," said the Major.

"Meaning that you could take them. Then, following, move up on the Round Tops, gaining the high ground that overlooks the Union position. If you take that, the whole of Meade's flank will be exposed and vulnerable."

"I doubt that General Meade would make such a mistake," said the Major.

Dennison looked at him. He knew where the battle was

going the next day because he had read the history books. He knew how the Rebels could win. He had all the answers and it looked like he wasn't going to be able to convince them. They would look at his information, convince themselves that the Yankees wouldn't be that dumb and then ignore it.

"General Meade won't make the mistake," said Dennison. "It's going to be made for him. The corps commander, General Sickles, is not a professional soldier. He doesn't fully understand the importance of guarding his flanks. That gives you, here, the chance to destroy him."

The Major looked at the map, seeing how the high ground was distributed. The last observations that had been made of the Union lines showed that there wasn't much in the south. A lot of rough ground to cover, but if they could get up to the Round Tops, it would give them a real advantage.

"A feint in the north," said Dennison, "would hold their attention there. Then when the assault came in the south, they wouldn't be ready for it."

For a long time, the Major studied the map. He had the lieutenant sketch in the position of the Union troops as Dennison had given them. Then he stepped back, a hand on his chin and let his eyes take in the big picture.

Then, almost as if talking to himself, he said, "If the intelligence is right, we can destroy the Union position by simply taking the Round Tops."

"The information is accurate," said Dennison. "You'll never know what I had to do to get it, but it is accurate. You now hold the key to the battle."

"I'll have to get this to General Longstreet," said the Major. "He may want to confer with you so I'll want you to stay here. Wait here."

Dennison smiled and moved to a small, wooden chair.

He sat down and brushed at some imagined dirt on the leg of his pants. "I'll be happy to wait. I'm sure that General Longstreet will know what to do with the intelligence."

The Major turned and pointed at one of the officers who had been hovering around the edge of the main group. "Lieutenant, I want you to ride over to General Longstreet. He's with General Hood right now, and tell him what we have here. You make sure that he knows the intelligence came from a single source, but it seems to be good."

"Yes sir."

"Find out what the General wants to do with it. And report back here."

"Yes sir."

Dennison watched the young officer disappear through the door. He had done it, he decided. Given them the information and they were going to act on it.

TWENTY-FOUR

David Jackson looked at the chronometer that was centered in the panel and watched as it snapped off the seconds until it turned over the hour. It was now nearly seven in the morning and as near as he could tell, it would be another nine hours before the travelers had the chance to make their change. He sat down, pressed a couple of buttons and then threw a switch on the console that seemed to wrap around him like the instrument panel of a jumbo jet. There were four positions on the console, three for the technicians and one for the supervisor. Normally, Jackson was on his feet behind them, moving from station to station, but tonight he sat there where he could watch the sensors. Just above him was the window that looked down on the bowl-shaped transfer chamber.

The control room itself was brightly lighted, carpeted with a static free rug, and painted in muted colors. There were no pictures on the walls, but there were checklists, detailing who to call in the event of an emergency, various techniques for handling those emergencies, and responses to anticipated problems. The room was squared on three sides and bowed inward on the fourth. The control panel was built in there. The panel contained four computer keyboards and monitors, various power controls, and switches that controlled everything from the transfer chamber to the lights in the conference room. The panel itself was made of brushed, stainless steel and loaded with access panels.

Out of the corner of his eye as he sat there, Jackson saw the Nazi commander push one of the technicians out of a chair and then sit down himself. Jackson turned. He could see into the conference room where the majority of his people were still being held. There was a single guard, holding an automatic weapon, standing in the doorway that separated the conference room from the control booth. He knew there were other guards, he just couldn't see them.

"What's taking so long?" demanded the Nazi officer.

Jackson turned back to his board, studying the Transfer coordinate indicator and the cross-temporal locater. The wavy lines dancing across the light blue screen told him a great deal, but to the Nazi he said, "There is a problem with the location. Since there is no stimulation of the locator, I have to manually search the various temporal locations and the ionic indicators are not active yet. That makes the search nearly impossible because I'm dealing with living entities who will not occupy the pre-designated retrieval point until much later."

"That sounds quite dramatic," said the Nazi. He reached out and grabbed a handful of Sarah's brown hair, jerking her head back. "How about if I just take this young lady out and shoot her. Think that might help you find the travelers?"

Jackson felt his stomach turn to ice. His eyes went wide

and his mouth went dry. He tried to speak, couldn't find the words, forced himself to swallow and tried again. "You can shoot, shoot everyone and it won't help me. I'm trying to lock onto a signal but it takes time."

The Nazi pulled on Sarah's hair hard, dragging her from her chair and forcing her to knee walk to him. He smiled at her, shoving her face down so that it was inches from his crotch. He heard her whimpering, deep in her throat, but she didn't speak.

"I may just kill her anyway," said the man. "Make you understand how serious we are."

"Please," Jackson said, his voice thin and tight. "Please. That won't help. We're doing everything we can, but this isn't an exact science yet. We're still experimenting."

The Nazi pushed Sarah away from him so that she fell to her side. She froze there, afraid to move, her eyes staring at the Nazi's boots. She sniffed once and was silent.

"Get up, bitch," he said. "Get back to work, but if you look at me cross-eyed, I'll kill you."

Slowly she got to her feet and took her chair at the console. She hadn't been so scared since the Nazi had punched her in the stomach hours ago. Not so scared since she had thought he was going to rape her. Now, through a blur of tears, she tried to study the electromagnetic sensors in front of her. She raised a shaking hand to her cheek, brushed her hair off her face and then leaned forward.

The Nazi got to his feet and stepped to the doorway so that he could look into the conference room. He let his eyes roam over the people being held hostage there. Jackson had demanded that twelve of them be released to help him, but the others still sat there, hands bound behind them, waiting for the other shoe to fall. The Nazi wondered if he shouldn't take five of them out to be shot, as an incentive to Jackson.

Sarah slid across the floor in her chair using the wheels on it. She stopped next to Jackson and whispered. "I think I've got an indication on—"

Without looking at her, he hissed under his breath, "Kill it. Lose it."

"What . . . ?"

The Nazi spun and leaped forward, sticking his face between them. "What are you two talking about?"

"Fluctuation in the power grids that are indicative of the transfer field collapsing."

"What the fuck does that mean?"

"It means," said Jackson, "that we're losing all contact with the travelers."

"You told me that you had no contact with them," roared the Nazi. "You told me that you had no idea where they were."

Jackson held up a hand as if warding off a blow. "When I said that we didn't have contact with them, I meant that we didn't know exactly where they were," he said hastily. "We know *when* they are and we're losing that fix."

The Nazi turned and slapped Sarah. "Get them back. You lose them and I'm going to kill everyone here."

Jackson looked at the clock. Only another twelve minutes had passed. There was no way he could delay everything for several more hours without the Nazi going berserk. More people were going to die. He put his hands to his face and then rubbed his eyes, feeling tired. Tired and sick. He took a deep breath and said, "This isn't going to work."

"You better make it work," demanded the Nazi.

"I can't." Jackson rocked back in his chair and then turned so that he was facing the enemy soldier. "I could sit here until the middle of next year and there is no guarantee that I'll be able to find them."

"Then people will die. I don't have much time left."

"There is an alternative," said Jackson. "A way for you to complete your mission."

"What's that?"

"Send some of your own people back. Send them to Gettysburg to stop the travelers from making their changes. We can still work to find the travelers, but at the same time your men could be trying to stop them."

The Nazi was quiet for a moment, thinking. Then he said, "Won't work. My men wouldn't know where to look or who they were."

"Wouldn't matter," said Jackson. "We can tell you everything you need to know so that your men could find them."

"Doctor Jackson," shouted Sarah, "You can't do that!"

"Shut up, Sarah," shouted Jackson right back. "I can do that and I will. There are other things that have to be considered. Lives are at stake."

Again the Nazi stepped close to her, doubling his fist. He smiled as she shrank back, her eyes wide in fright. She looked like she was going to say something and then thought better of it. The Nazi grinned and watching her, said, "How long would it take to set up?"

"Thirty minutes. Couple of minutes to brief your people and instruct them on the recall system. Call it forty-five minutes on the outside."

"How many men?"

"Two. Three. Whatever you think," said Jackson.

"Then let's get started."

"You pick your men. Sarah, start the initial transfer procedure."

"Doctor—"

"Just do it."

"Yes sir."

Jackson turned to the console, flipped a couple of

switches that locked in the spacio-time coordinates. Threw in the Decca Nav system that provided a lock on the proper location. That was a refinement that Tucker didn't have. A way of moving the people to the proper location as they traveled through time. A computer program provided a compensation for the rotation of the Earth and it's journey through the galaxy. Without it, the time traveler was locked into the location where he started the trip.

Jackson spoke out loud, directing his comments at the Nazi. "Since we've already sent people into this period, the preliminaries won't take nearly as long as setting up for a new shoot."

"I'm not at all interested in this."

"Fine," said Jackson. He let his hand slide up the console, to a small black wheel that looked like the flap controls on some aircraft, and spun it. As the LED numbers in a dial began to rotate, Jackson hit another button and zeroed the counter. As he did that, he glanced at Sarah who stared at him, her mouth open. When it looked like she was going to say something, Jackson just winked at her. She raised her eyebrows, but turned back to her work.

"Who you going to send?" asked Jackson.

The Nazi stepped to the door and said, "Scmidt, Heinz. In here."

Two men, both dressed in the black SS uniforms, entered. They snapped to attention and waited. Jackson hesitated, wondering if their leader was going to say anything to them, and when he didn't, Jackson said, "You'll want to find a small contingent of people on the hill known as Little Round Top."

He was going to say more and then realized that the Nazis probably didn't teach their soldiers about the American Civil War. He got to his feet and started for the conference room.

"Where the hell do you think you're going?"

"Map," said Jackson. "A map to show them what they need to know about the battle. So they'll know where our people are."

"Hurry."

Jackson entered the conference room and headed for the closet hidden behind one of the wall panels. He pushed on it and stepped back as it popped open. He took a rolled map from the corner and returned to the control room.

There, he unrolled the map and spread it out. Pointing, he said, "Union lines are here, along Cemetery Ridge. Rebels are over here, a thousand yards away. Now, I'll set you down on the evening of the first day, behind Little Round Top. All you'll have to do is climb the hill, it's fairly short, and the people you find on the top will be the travelers. Escort them off the hill. That'll preserve everything."

The Nazi leader moved forward, staring at the map. When Jackson finished his briefing, the man said, "When you find them, kill them."

"Now wait a minute," said Jackson. "I'm not going to send your men into the past to kill . . ."

"You will do as ordered or I will start shooting the people in the conference room. You decide. Which will it be?"

Jackson said, "Tom, take these men to the transfer chamber and get them ready. Signal as soon as you're done."

Tom didn't move for a moment. Then he got to his feet, stared at Jackson with hate-filled eyes and growled at the men. "Come with me."

As they left the control room Sarah said, "Doctor Jackson, I don't think—"

"Don't worry about it," said Jackson. "I've got it covered. Everything is covered."

The Nazi's head snapped around and he thrust his face at Sarah. "What don't you?"

"I . . . I—"

"Come on! Speak up girl! What don't you?"

She looked at Jackson, afraid to say anything. She didn't know what was happening. Jackson was violating procedure. And she couldn't believe the way he was helping the Nazis. There were too many things that she just didn't understand. Too many variables that made no sense. She decided that playing dumb was the best way to go.

"I don't like this. We're helping you kill our own people. Helping you to—"

The Nazi reached out and patted her cheek. "Think of it this way. You're helping yourself save your own life. If you make me angry, I may just take you out and shoot you."

She turned back to the console and reached for a switch with a hand that was shaking. She was going to say something, and then decided that she would just sit there and do a little as possible.

The Nazi turned and stared at Jackson, watching him work. He reached out, put a hand on the console and said, "You caved in to that pretty easy. My men are going to kill yours."

Jackson knew that he had reached a moment of truth. If he misplayed the hand, many people were going to die. He glanced at the Nazi, held his eyes for a second and then dropped his. For a moment, he didn't speak. Then quietly, as if talking to himself, said, "They aren't my people. I only met them once."

The Nazi threw back his head and laughed. "You people are all alike. Kill a hundred, a thousand and as long as you don't know them, you don't care. Those people are humans too, Jackson."

There was nothing Jackson could say. He knew exactly what he was doing and had to play it just right. He kept his eyes on the floor and didn't move.

"How long before we know if they were successful?" said the Nazi, the contempt thick in his voice.

Jackson shrugged, but didn't look up. "Can't say. As soon as your men have completed their task, they activate the wrist control that Tom will give them. At that moment we'll retrieve them."

"How long?"

"Couple of hours at the most, " said Jackson. "It'll take that long for them to get into the proper position to complete their mission."

The light went on in the transfer chamber and a small red lamp glowed on the control panel. Jackson got to his feet and leaned forward so that he could look into the chamber. He saw the two men, holding their ugly, squat weapons, standing in the center of the chamber. Both were looking around as if searching for a way to escape.

The red light on the panel went out and Jackson said, "We're ready here."

"Then do it," said the Nazi.

Jackson took a key from his pocket and unlocked a small box that was fastened under the console. He took another key from there and put it into the console and turned it one position to the right. He glanced at Sarah and nodded at her.

She took a notebook from the rack near her and opened to the first page that was encased in acetate. She took a felt tip marker from the breast pocket of her safety-pinned coverall and said, "Main Temporal Sequence activated."

"Yes," said Jackson. He twisted a knob and flipped a series of switches near him. "Set one. Ready for level six."

Sarah checked it off her list and said, "Power supply to full tap."

Jackson looked at a dial and said, "Set to full tap."

"Coming up on power level and five minutes," said Sarah, checking the dials arranged to her left. "Initiate main sequence."

"Main Sequence initiated. Cross over to level seven."

Sarah reached to the right, flipped a switch and then watched as the technician next to her ran through a series of checks, looking at the warning lights on his panel and snapping switches with his thumb. When he finished, he nodded.

"Cross-over completed."

"Power levels at the ready."

"Okay," said Jackson, "we can forget the checklist now." He twisted the key to the second position and said, "We're at level eight. Activate temporal lock."

"Lock activated," said Sarah. She looked at the LED in front of her, blinked and said, "Doctor Jackson, we've got . . ."

"Lock activated," Jackson cut in. "Sarah, I know what I'm doing, thank you."

"Sorry, Doctor."

Jackson ignored that and said, "Seal the temporal chamber and sound hallway alarm."

The technician pushed a button, waited a moment and pushed a second button. "Chamber sealed."

"Ah, Doctor," said Sarah again, her eyes still on the LED in front of her. "I have—"

"If you can't follow the sequence," snapped Jackson, "I will have you removed. Now. I have a green board."

"Green board," said the technician.

"Green board," said Sarah, "with a—"

"Green boards all around," said Jackson, cutting her off

for the third time. "Prepare to launch." He turned the key to the last position and before Sarah could protest again, he hit the button and said, "Launch."

Behind the window there was a burst of bright light and then a golden glow that seemed to solidify near the ceiling and then slowly descend over the men in the chamber. They sparkled for a moment and vanished.

Jackson turned his key back to the first position and pulled it from the lock. He put it into the lock box and then leaned back, lacing his fingers behind his head. He looked at the Nazi commander and said, "That's got it. Your people are on their way to Gettysburg."

The Nazi looked suspiciously from Jackson to Sarah and back again. He felt that something about the trip was not quite right, but wasn't sure what it was. He pointed at Sarah and said, "What was bothering you?"

She looked at Jackson, as if for help, but before she could speak, one of the other Nazis burst into the room. He leaned close to his commander's ear, whispering quickly and excitedly.

"You know what to do," the commander said. "You tell Lieutenant Schultz to take five hostages to the front of the building so that the security forces can see them. You let it be known they will die if anyone rushes the building. You tell them we want safe passage out of here."

"Yes sir."

The Nazi climbed to his feet and moved to the door, looking into the conference room. He turned back and said, "I want you to keep searching for your travelers. Maybe with the added incentive of them being killed if my men find them first, you'll try a little harder."

Jackson shrugged and said, "I don't see how we can work any faster than we have." He glanced at the clock and saw that the launch of the two Nazi soldiers had eaten another hour and twelve minutes from the time left before the change was made. Still a long time, but with the Nazi commander placated, and their own security forces surrounding the building, Jackson thought that they would be safe now. He didn't think the Nazis would shoot anyone else. All he had to do was wait patiently and let the Nazis think that his plan would work.

The two Nazis, Scmidt and Heinz, stood on an open plain that stretched for miles. A short, dirty-looking grass covered the plain. The sun, a hazy, red orb hung in the sky near the horizon, above the single tree that was visible. A gigantic herd of animals, brown, shaggy beasts that were six or seven feet tall at the shoulder, surrounded the tree. Overhead a cloud of pink birds wheeled, screeching at one another.

Heinz turned slowly, taking in everything that he could see. Open prairie for miles in all directions. Low hills to the south and nothing else. There were no people. No buildings. No soldiers about to engage in a great conflict.

Neither Heinz nor Scmidt knew that they were the only two men to ever see the animals in front of them. Animals that would be extinct long before the first of their human ancestors began to walk upright. The fossil record contained no evidence of the beasts since they would live and die in a climate that did not produce fossils.

Scmidt cocked his weapon nervously and turned. "I believe we have been played for the fools."

Heinz nodded his agreement and touched the control around his wrist, unaware that it was not a working model. It had been given to him for show. And it did not have the several million years of range that it would have needed anyway.

TWENTY-FIVE

The morning dawned partly cloudy but the heat of the day before had not been chased by the night. Even at six it was uncomfortable and Kent found that sitting up was enough to make him sweat. He climbed to his feet and surveyed the area in front of him. There wasn't much change from the night before. He could still see the Union lines stretched out to the north. It seemed that someone had taken the time to examine them and then order the units about, solidifying the line, strengthening it and consolidating it. There were cannon emplacements behind the Union positions, facing the Confederate units on Seminary Ridge and on the eastern side of Emmitsburg Road. Although he couldn't see any Rebels in the trees over there, he was sure that they had taken positions in them.

He stretched, his fists high over his head, and was slightly upset by the popping of his joints. He was getting too old to spend the night sleeping on the ground, eating

165

food out of a can heated over open fires, and brushing his teeth with salt. He stepped forward and found Brown sitting on a gigantic boulder, his binoculars to his eyes.

"Today's critical," said Brown when he heard Kent approach. "Today we find out what's going on."

Kent ran a hand through his tangled hair and then sat down. He blinked rapidly and then rubbed his eyes, digging the grit out of them. "So what *is* going on?"

Brown lowered his binoculars and pointed. "We got somebody out there, in front of us. I think it's Sickles' Corps. If I remember right, the major part of the battle will take place in front of us starting late in the afternoon. They'll be skirmishing and fucking around all morning."

Below him, in the broken ground that hid the Devil's Den, the wheatfield and the Peach Orchard, Kent could see nothing. The soldiers down there had formed a skirmish line and had taken a defensive position. He knew they were down there, he just couldn't see them.

Then, forgetting about that, Kent said, "The one piece of information that we haven't been given is who in the hell made the first change?" Kent thought about what he had said and added, "Somewhere along the line, the Rebels have to get a piece of information that allows them to shift their forces. If no one interferes, then history follows the course we know. If someone does, then we have the problems that have arisen."

Brown looked to the rear, where the majority of the mercenaries slept. "I thought that Maddie said something about a ripple effect. Or you did. Someone did. Would that account for the problems?"

"I can't see it," said Kent. "We appear in 1836 and suddenly the Union loses at Gettysburg. No ripple. This has to be an out and out attempt by someone to change the course of history."

"You sure?"

Kent smiled and chuckled. "No, I'm not sure. I'm guessing but I still believe Newton was right. For every action there is an equal and opposite reaction. I can't see how our appearance in 1836 is the action that creates the reaction in 1863. There has to be something else."

"What brought this up?" asked Brown.

"I've been thinking about it," said Kent. "You've been sitting here telling us what's going to happen. Everything that you learned about the battle has been right. Now, sometime today, something is going to change. There has to be a cause for it."

"Okay," said Brown. "I believe that. So what do we do about it?"

"We've got the high ground where the change is going to take place. We know what's going to happen here. I would suggest that someone from our side try to convince one of the Union generals to put someone up here now. A company. A regiment. Then someone else or all of us should scatter along the line and see if we can figure out what is going on."

"I don't know," said Brown. "Seems that the change is made here when one of Longstreet's brigades makes an end run and takes Little Round Top. We stay put and repel that, we've won the day."

"If that is the only problem," said Kent.

"I've looked at the history that Maddie provided and it seems to me that the critical mistake or rather change, is made right here."

"Granted," said Kent. "Except that I'm not convinced that we should take everything she says as the gospel."

Brown turned and stared at Kent. He raised his eyebrows in question and said, "That's an interesting thing to say, considering everything that happened last night. You two have become fast friends."

"Yes, well," he said. "I'm only saying that it seems that there is something else going on. Something that we've not been told about. As long as the battle develops along the lines you remember, I'd say that we're in the clear, but if something new crops up, then we'd better talk. Re-evaluate the situation before we make a mistake ourselves."

"Are you saying that you don't trust her?"

"I'm saying that we should keep an eye on the situation and be prepared to react to the changing conditions. Maybe keep an eye on her."

"So you don't trust her."

"Trust has nothing to do with it, Colonel."

Somewhere to the right there was a sudden burst of firing. Cannons boomed. To the front, along Seminary Ridge there was an eruption of smoke and flame. There were individual clouds of smoke billowing from rifles that quickly combined with others until part of the valley was obscured in a soft blue fog. Brown climbed to the top of the rock, watched for a moment, but then the firing died.

As Brown jumped down, he said, "Just the two sides feeling each other out."

There was a noise behind them and both turned to look. Maddie, Cunningham and a couple of the mercenaries stood there. Cunningham hitchhiked a thumb over his shoulder and said, "Big bunch of people coming up."

Brown looked at the sun, tried to guess the time and said, "That'll be Sykes' Fifth Corps. They'll deploy just to the north of here along the Taneytown Road."

"I'm tired of hearing about this, Colonel," said Kent. "I don't want to know what's going to happen or what's supposed to happen. I think we're making a mistake. I think that we should do something now to ensure that the battle goes as it is supposed to and then get the hell out of here."

"So what do you suggest?" asked Brown.

Kent glanced at the others for support, saw them standing there with blank looks on their faces. He hesitated and then said, "Tell Meade what is going to happen. Tell his generals. Sitting here is not the answer."

For a moment, Brown didn't speak. He stared at his men and then turned to study the broken terrain in front of him. Finally he said, "I think you may be right. Let's get some breakfast and then we'll see what we can do to convince the people around here to make some changes."

Brown ate a cold meal, not wanting to bother with heating it over the fire that Kent and Cunningham built. When he finished, he gave orders to a number of the men, telling them who to see and what they should say. He told McGee to find General Warren because it was Warren who ended up on Little Round Top. He told Peter Baily to find General Sickles to let him know that his divisions had been badly deployed.

Brown smiled as he said that, and added, "But be a little more diplomatic than that. Suggest to him that he has his flanks anchored in the air and should be pulled back slightly so that the Rebels can't run around his end."

"He's not going to listen to me."

"So tell him you're from Meade's headquarters. Once you explain the situation to him, he should see the mistake himself."

"Guess that makes sense," said Baily.

Brown looked at Cunningham and Kent. "What are your plans?"

"Thought that we'd move up to Cemetery Hill and watch the war from there."

"Good," said Brown. "Remember, the fighting there gets quite heavy so watch yourselves." He stopped talking and then added, "Oh, everyone. Let's try to get back here by three. The fighting will shift to here about that time."

"What about us?" asked Andross.

"Well," said Brown, "we'll want to leave some people up here. You and Meg and Maddie. Crawford, you stay here too along with Blair, Forsyth, Waters . . ." He waved a hand. "The rest of you. Deploy along the western side of the south slope and wait for the probe by the Rebels."

There were a few nods. Then, behind them, they heard a noise and turned. A squad of men lead by a Union lieutenant appeared. He held up a hand, stopping the men and stared at the people in front of him. "Who are you?" he demanded.

Brown stepped forward and said, "I'm Colonel Robert K. Brown and was sent up here for a reconnaissance of the Rebel lines."

The lieutenant brought his heels together and snapped off a salute. "Sorry, sir. We were told that there was no one up here. We're going to establish a signal post."

"Please carry on with your orders then," said Brown. "We'll try to stay out of your way."

"Yes sir," said the Lieutenant. "Thank you, sir." He pointed to the left and said, "All right, boys, you know what to do."

"If I may suggest, Lieutenant, place some of your men on the southwestern side of the hill. If a Rebel attack comes, it will be from that angle."

"Sir, my orders are to establish a signal position."

"I understand that, but you are a soldier first. I'm concerned about a possible Rebel attempt to take this hill, thereby giving them the high ground advantage. I am not suggesting that you abandon your orders, only that you assist my people in establishing a defensive line until more troops can be brought up."

"Yes sir. I will see to it."

"Good." Brown directed his attention to Kent and Cunningham. "You two had better get going. You have a lot of ground to cover. Remember to be back here by the middle of the afternoon."

"Yes sir," said Kent.

TWENTY-SIX

Dennison sat in the woods outside Longstreet's head-quarters and watched the sun rise. There was a light mist that drifted through the trees covering everything with moisture. Dennison felt sticky as the dew settled and wished that there was a way to take a shower or a bath. He knew that the sun would quickly burn off the mist and that he would wish that it was back.

Instead of waiting to eat, waiting for the sun to dry the landscape, Dennison swung back into the saddle and headed to Longstreet's HQ. There he learned that General Longstreet was conferring with General Lee at Lee's head-quarters. Dennison didn't wait for more because he knew that the critical decisions were being made. Decisions that would affect the outcome of the battle, and if he, Denni-son, could influence those decisions, then Gettysburg could become a Rebel victory.

Once again, as he approached, he was stopped by a

series of guards, but his letter did its job. Finally he was in front of a small, stone house with chimneys at both ends. There was a slight overhang that protected the front door, a tall picket fence near it and a trellis on the side holding up a flowering bush. A captain took Dennison inside and told him to wait.

Through the door that led to another room, Dennison could hear the men arguing. He recognized Lee's voice as it cut through the sound like a knife. "I'm not going to wait for General Meade to attack. I'm going to hit him. Take the battle to him."

"Yes sir," said a voice that sounded like Longstreet. "I think we should, but I don't think that the attack should come in the north. Let me hit him all along the front here."

The voices suddenly dropped to a mumble and then the officer was back. "You may go in."

Dennison entered the room and wondered if there was someone mass-producing them. He saw a stone fireplace, a table with chairs near it and a map tacked to the wall. It looked like the one he had been in with Longstreet the night before.

General Lee sat in a wing-back chair, his face nearly as gray as his uniform. There were dark circles under his eyes that contrasted to the white of his hair and beard. He sat quietly for a moment, almost as if he had gone to sleep and then looked up expectantly. "What do you have for us, Mr. Harrison?"

Dennison was taken aback by the name and then remembered it was the one he had chosen for himself days before when he had thought it was a good idea. He shook his head, walked to the map and said, "I can tell you everything that you want to know about the Yankee lines. Without General Stuart around here for reconnaissance, I may be the only source you have."

Lee nodded and waved a hand. "Quickly. Tell us."

"The Yankee line is most vulnerable around the south end. An attack there will roll up the flanks of one of the Corps. I'm not sure which one, but their commander hasn't placed his troops well. You have the opportunity to dislodge him. Take the high ground away from him."

"And on the north?" asked General Lee.

"Forget about the north. Hit it with a diversionary attack to keep Meade from shifting his men and you'll soon find that Meade will have to withdraw or surrender."

Lee snapped his fingers and pointed at a pitcher of water. He was handed a glass, drank and then said, "You seem very sure of yourself, Mr. Harrison."

"Yes sir. I have spent the night studying the Yankee lines from all angles. They are weak here, on the south, and an attack will destroy their flank."

Lee got to his feet and moved to the map. He studied it and then said, "Thank you for your help, Mr. Harrrison. Please wait outside while I confer with my officers."

Dennison spent a tense hour pacing in the front room. He wanted to press his ear against the wall, to listen in, but was afraid that someone would see him in that position and think he was spying on General Lee. And, of course, that was exactly what he would be doing. Except it was to make sure that Lee and his generals understood the importance of the intelligence he had given them. He had handed them the victory, if they were smart enough to see it.

When the door opened, Dennison leaped to his feet. Longstreet came out and said, "I want you to come with me."

"Yes sir," said Dennison. "What about General Lee?"

"Don't worry about him. He has decided to follow your

advice. I want to thank you for that. You swayed him to my position." Longstreet smiled. At least it looked as if he tried to smile. "He changed his mind three or four times, but he finally decided to let my Corps lead the assault. Ewell and his people will create the diversion."

Dennison felt a thrill ripple through him. He wanted to leap into the air, he wanted to shout and dance and laugh. Instead, he tried to maintain a stoic look and said simply, "Good. Now we'll kick some Yankee butt."

"That we will," said Longstreet. "Come along to my headquarters and we'll take a look at the map. You can show me what you consider the best routes for the attack."

"Wouldn't some of your officers be better suited for that?" asked Dennison.

"Don't get me wrong. They will check all routes of attack. I just want your advice about it so that we'll know where to look."

"Yes sir. No problem."

And there hadn't been a problem with that. Dennison had laid out an assault route that would run around the end of Sickles' Corps and crush it. That would give the Rebels the high ground. But then the delays started. The shifting of the troops took time. The readjustment of the artillery took time. The issuing of the orders to the various field units took time. The recall and the new battlelines took time to set up. The requests of the commanders took more time.

Dennison rode among the troops, watching them. They seemed to be a happy bunch unconcerned about the coming battle. They were joking with each other, eating a noon meal, cleaning their equipment or writing letters. Many were trying to find a little shade as the sun reached its zenith, baking the ground and the men. Many had taken off their coats so that they weren't the long gray lines, but a ragtag-looking group.

At one o'clock, Dennison ran out of patience. He had thought that Longstreet was about to attack hours earlier. Had assumed as he and Longstreet left the last of the staff meetings that the assault would begin in no more than an hour. Now it was afternoon and there was still no sign that the Rebels were close to attacking.

He had heard firing as skirmishers from both armies stumbled across each other. There were counter-battery duels as the artillerymen from both sides tried to destroy the cannon of the other. There were troops shifting around, sliding into new positions, out of sight of the enemy soldiers. But there was not the full-scale attack that he had expected. He was getting nervous about it because he knew that every second the Rebels delayed gave the Union that much more time to prepare.

Dennison headed back to Longstreet's headquarters. By this time, the guards knew who it was and he had no trouble passing them. Inside the farmhouse, he confronted Longstreet, telling the General that he had to make a move quickly.

Longstreet, who was seated at a desk, looked up at Dennison as if he had just made an obnoxious noise and asked, "Who in the hell put you in charge, sir?"

Dennison stood his ground and said, "If we don't attack soon, General, the Yankees will be ready and the day will be lost."

Longstreet put the cap back on his pen, set it on the desk and said, "I'll tell you what. You ride over to General McLaw's division and wait there with him for his orders to begin the attack." Longstreet reached out and pulled a watch toward him, checking the time. "Within the hour."

"Yes General," said Dennison. "But please remember that the critical assault will be around the end, toward the Round Tops." He was going to protest that he would be more valuable with the troops assaulting the flank, but knew that a good, solid attack on the front of Sickles' Corps would draw reinforcements there, giving the troops on the flank a better chance at success.

Dennison rode out again, found the headquarters of McLaw's division. He was becoming frustrated. He knew the answers, knew how to save the battle, and couldn't get anyone to act. They all fucked around, moving troops back and forth, waiting, arguing and then starting another round of moving the troops.

It was nearly four o'clock when he found McLaw's headquarters. Just as he reined up there was a series of booms from far behind him and then explosions in the Peach Orchard. Dennison saw the mushrooming clouds of dirt and debris and the red orange flashes of fire. He slipped from the saddle and stood holding the reins, watching as the second volley slammed into the trees. There was some answering fire from Union positions on Cemetery Ridge, but that didn't slow the Confederate bombardment.

Then finally, Dennison saw the beginning of the assault. Thousands of men from General Hood's division began to advance, at first slowly until they had their lines formed and then rapidly, across the broken ground and through the trees. There was some scattered resistance from Union skirmishers but they were overrun quickly by the Rebels.

Dennison watched, fascinated for a moment, and then leaped onto his horse and rode to the top of the high ground where he could watch the battle develop. He saw the men from Hood's division reach Plum Run at the foot of the Round Tops. He wanted to shout because it looked as if the plan was going to work. The Rebels now had their troops in a position to crush the Yankee resistance and roll up the flank.

TWENTY-SEVEN

After he had talked to his people, Brown had worked his way down the broken, rock-strewn slopes of Little Round Top to wander behind Sickles' lines. He knew what was coming and wanted to see it. In fact, he knew quite a bit about Gettysburg and had spent the day trying to get the overall picture. The task proved impossible because he was limited in what he could see and what he could learn. Messages were passed by horsemen and runners, not by radio. To travel the full length of the Union lines would take a couple of hours, if he was going to avoid being shot at by the Rebels.

He got behind a Union brigade and followed it as it moved through the Peach Orchard toward the Emmitsburg Road. When it halted and began to form a line, Brown found a place for himself. No one questioned him because he wore the eagles of a Union colonel and everyone assumed that he had been assigned to the brigade as an observer. Brown thought that if he had such sloppy security, he would have fired a couple of people.

The first explosion, deep in the trees and somewhere behind him, caught him by surprise. Like a recruit, Brown turned to see what had blown up and then realized that it was artillery falling on his position. He dived for cover, rolling next to a tree. Not ideal, but better than the open, especially if the Rebels began using shot cannisters.

Brown scrambled around the tree so that he could see the Emmitsburg Road and the Rebel positions beyond it. Even in the late afternoon sun, he saw the bright flashes as the cannons fired from the high ground of Seminary Ridge. He heard the thundering of the cannon shells as they roared overhead. He turned once and saw the detonation in the rear of the formation. A geyser of debris, dirt and dust thrown into the air, bits of it trailing smoke. He heard the shouts of the men around it, some screaming in pain, others with fright.

Then Brown remembered that this was the Civil War and not Vietnam. In America's last war, it had been right for the officers to seek shelter during bombardment. If they didn't, they were relieved for insanity. But here, in the Civil War, the officers were supposed to be out front, leading the men, ignoring the danger to themselves. They were supposed to stand up during the cannonade and show the men that it wasn't that frightening. In fact, for the first few years, officers weren't even eligible to win the Medal of Honor because any and all acts of bravery by them were considered line of duty.

Brown climbed to his feet and stood next to the tree. He heard another cannonball overhead, ducked but called out, "Be brave, my boys. Be brave." He realized that he sounded like some of the quotes he had read. Officers who said dumb things in the heat of battle.

Then it seemed that the orchard was erupting in flame, smoke and fire. The ground shook and rumbled and the leaves fell from the trees like it was autumn. Brown could hear the dirt cascading down from the explosions, rattling through the trees like a summer shower. There was shouting around him, men in panic and pain, while others used their rifles in an ineffectual response.

Brown wished he had a sword. All the heroic pictures he had seen of the Civil War had officers leading their men, rallying their men, with their swords held high. He whipped his hat from his head and waved it in the air.

"Steady men. Steady. The enemy is only trying to soften us up for the attack."

There was a sudden, inexplicable lull in the firing and a single voice shouted back, "I'm pretty soft already."

That was answered by a chorus of cheers and Brown knew that the men around him would remain in place, even as the artillery began to fall again. Then there was a rising shout, a yelling as thousands of men burst from the trees on the other side of Emmitsburg Road. A long gray line of men partially obscured by the smoke and dust of the artillery fire.

Around him, Brown heard men screaming, "Here they come! Here they come!" and the officers running along the Yankee lines telling the men, "Hold your fire!" The Union soldiers were surging forward, finding cover behind the trees, a piece of a fence, depressions in the ground or behind bushes. They formed a long rank, their rifles leveled. Each had a bayonet fixed to it and they sparkled in the sun, almost as if inviting the Rebels closer.

No one ever really gave the command to fire. All at once, the line erupted. A thousand rifles fired, spitting smoke and flame. There was a long, drawn-out thunderclap as the cloud created by the rifles rolled forward, toward the onrushing Rebels. For an instant, they were hidden by the wall of blue and as it slowly raised, Brown could see a hundred dead men littering the field.

The Union soldiers got to their feet, the only way that they could reload. There was a scramble as each of them used his ramrod, then dug at his bullet pouch and tried to pour the powder and shot into the barrel of his weapon. Brown watched as the men worked. He could see them all sweating now, not all of it from the heat of the afternoon. He heard the men grumbling under their breath, cursing clumsy fingers and lousy designs.

And then, all at once, it seemed that the Union line was ready again. There was a rippling of shot and then a massive explosion as nearly everyone pulled the trigger at the same time. The Rebels vanished behind a wall of smoke and then burst through it, nearly on top of the Union position.

Brown, on one knee, fired his weapon slowly, picking the targets carefully. He saw dust fly from the uniforms as the men toppled to the ground. He flipped one man back and thought that he heard him scream in pain. He fired one last time and watched as the man fell forward, rolled over and then sat up holding on to his leg. The wounded man was close enough that Brown could see the blood bubbling between his fingers.

Before he could fire again, the Rebels were overrunning his position. A man came at him, his bayonet extended. The Rebel thrust. Brown parried it easily, pushing the bayonet to the side and came up with the butt of his weapon. He slammed it into the chin of the enemy and then brought the barrel around, the bayonet slicing into the gray coat of the Rebel, drawing blood. The enemy fell unconscious.

As Brown fought a second Rebel, this one more experienced with the bayonet, he noticed that the Union line was sagging badly. Brown turned, swung at the man, missed and felt a stab of pain on his arm as the enemy cut him. Brown jumped back, seemed to stumble and as the Rebel followed, Brown attacked. The man parried and tried to swing the butt of his rifle into Brown's face. Brown dropped to one knee and kicked out with a foot, knocking the man off his feet. As he landed on his back, Brown thrust once, driving the bayonet into the man's stomach. There was a shriek of pain and the man grabbed the barrel of Brown's weapon. Brown yanked it free and the man cut his hands on the blood-dripping blade.

Around him the defense of the Peach Orchard was collapsing. More Rebels were crossing the road as the commanders there committed everything they had. Brown turned and saw men in blue uniforms, their weapons thrown away, running for the shelter of Little Round Top. Brown saw the other men wavering.

He yelled, "Steady! Steady! Fall back slowly. Let's fall back slowly."

The men began a gradual retreat, letting the Rebels push them. They fought on, bayonet against bayonet. There was sporadic firing into the Rebel lines. Brown saw that some of the Union officers had formed a skirmish line and ordered the men around him to run for that. As they approached, the Yankees opened fire, dropping dozens of the Rebels and halting their advance.

Brown raced through the line then. He stopped and looked back. Scattered among the trees were hundreds of bodies from both armies. Rebel and Yankee dead lying on top of one another, next to one another, so close that Brown could have walked through the Peach Orchard and never had to set foot on the ground, just as history demanded.

Even as the firing around him tapered, Brown heard the

roar of shooting from the Devil's Den. He was tempted to head over there to watch, because this too was important to the Union cause. It was this pressure on the Union southern flank that would or could lead to the Rebel victory. He knew that as long as the Union held Little Round Top, the flank would be protected.

He turned and saw movement on the top of it and then saw a line of enemy soldiers advancing up the southern side. He knew that the men in the Devil's Den had been flanked.

He ran to the rear and stopped near one of the Union generals. He pulled the binoculars from their case and surveyed the Rebel assault. They were taking some heavy rifle and cannon fire. He looked to the summit of Little Round Top and saw that someone had gotten a few cannon up there and at least a company of Union soldiers. That meant that one of his messengers had been successful.

As he slowly looked back to the west he saw a number of Rebel soldiers appear. The sun was behind them, silhouetting them. He watched them advance slowly. He turned his attention to the officers on horseback. He thought that he recognized one of them, having seen his picture in a dozen books about Gettysburg. And then he saw something that drained the blood from his face and made his stomach turn over.

He wanted to shout at the men with him, but knew that none of them would understand. He put the binoculars to his eyes again and studied the man to make sure that he was right. It had only been months since he had seen him the last time, although the man appeared to have aged thirty years.

Without a thought, he tossed his binoculars to the ground and heard them shatter. He raised his rifle, aiming at the man and pulled the trigger. He felt the rifle buck against his shoulder, saw the smoke flash from the barrel. He watched the target, but saw no reaction from it.

Again he aimed, but this time his weapon didn't fire. He cocked it again, but before he could shoot, he lost sight of the enemy. He lowered his rifle, staring into the Peach Orchard where the man had vanished.

"That explains it," said Brown to himself. "Explains it all."

TWENTY-EIGHT

Lemuel Crawford crouched behind one of the boulders at the summit of Little Round Top and watched the battle below him. Two brigades of Confederate soldiers had smashed through the Union lines destroying the resistance there. He had watched as the enemy had attacked, and the Union soldiers hid, waiting for the enemy. There was some shooting by skirmishers, and a little artillery fire, but the Confederates kept coming.

The Rebels reached Plum Run and turned toward the Round Tops trying to avoid Sickles' flank. There was a moment when it looked bad, and then the Union soldiers opened fire with a single, brigade-sized volley. The Rebels hesitated, but came on just as the Yankees fired again. The enemy was confused and during that confusion, the Union attacked, driving them back.

Crawford crawled forward so that he could see better. He raised his rifle and fired into the mass of Rebel soldiers as they gathered for a counterattack. A moment later they began their assault, hitting the Union line and the fighting became hand-to-hand. Confederate General Hood threw more of his brigades into the battle, pushing the Union troops back. Crawford did what he could, firing into the Rebels as fast as he could pull the trigger.

Around him a small Union brigade began to infiltrate, taking up positions near the battery of cannon that had arrived only a while before. These men, ordered to Little Round Top by General Warren, had been involved in some of the earlier fighting. Warren recognized the real threat to the Union line and was fighting to get men to the high ground.

With the scrambling of the Union troops on the slopes of Little Round Top, the battle seemed to shift. Crawford watched as the Rebels began an assault up the hill. He knew that the critical phase of the battle had finally come. If the Union lost Little Round Top, then the flank would be overrun and the whole line would collapse.

As the Union troops ran along the slopes of the Little Round Top, Crawford had left his post and raced to join them. He slipped into the line as the two forces met and battle was joined. He used his rifle, picking off the enemy soldiers closest to him. He saw the men around him using their ramrods and digging at their ammo pouches. He saw one man load his weapon, fail to fire it and load it again. Crawford dropped behind a boulder near the man as he put a third load in the weapon, having yet to shoot it. Crawford became fascinated with the man, working so fast that he was forgetting the main step. Shooting at the enemy.

Now there were Rebels all around him. Crawford saw a standard-bearer running in the center of the line, his flag held high. Crawford aimed at him and fired. The man staggered, but kept running forward, almost as if he was unaware of the battle around him. Finally he fell to his knees, both hands on the flagpole, using it to support him. Crawford leaped over the boulder, ran forward and grabbed the battle flag.

The enemy soldier held on. He looked up at Crawford, his eyes slightly unfocused. Crawford jerked on the pole, but the man still clutched it, sprawling forward. Crawford took a step and then cocked a foot to kick the enemy in the head, but couldn't do it. He yanked again, jerking the flagpole from the Rebel's fist. The man rolled to his side, reached out, almost as if praying. Crawford stared at him as he coughed, blood spilling down over his lips and down his chin. He dropped his head to the ground, coughed again and seemed to sigh.

Crawford spun and ran back to the Union lines, hurdling over the boulder. He leaned back, breathing hard, holding the Confederate battle flag high. The men around him burst into cheering. Crawford had forgotten the importance of capturing the enemy's battle flags. The worst fate that could befall a regiment was to lose its colors. It was worse than being wiped out. In fact, it could be slaughtered to a man, but the honor of the regiment would be maintained, as long as the enemy didn't capture the colors.

But then the time for cheering passed and the enemy was attacking in force. The firing became a continual roar as the enemy vanished behind the smoke and flame of the weapons. Crawford found it hard to breathe, as if he was standing in the middle of a burning building. He could taste the bitter, acrid gunsmoke on his tongue. He tried to spit it out, but the air was so thick with it that it covered him.

He turned, saw an enemy soldier and shot him. A second one appeared and Crawford fired at him. Then the area was crawling with the enemy and the Union troops were running back up the hill. Crawford grabbed his flag, tried to roll it around the pole so that he wouldn't be shot by his own side, and scampered after them.

The fighting increased. There was more shooting. A roar from cannons. Crawford found a slight depression and dived into it. He rolled once, poked his weapon out and waited. It seemed that the firing became louder, one long, drawn-out peal of thunder that shook the world. Men were falling, almost dancing as if standing on a hot surface in bare feet. There was screaming and shouting and the sound of bugles all around. But the running stopped and the Union line found a position they could hold. They fired into the swarming Confederate lines, killing them. More soldiers dropped into bloody heaps. The ground under their feet, as the two sides mixed again, became red and muddy with blood. Men slipped in it, staining their uniforms, their boots, their hands. Men slashed at each other with swords, knives and bayonets.

Crawford lost sight of most of the battle around him. The smoke had become too thick and there was no breeze to blow it away. Crawford felt like a man in a fog. He could hear the battle but only see small parts of it. He climbed to his feet as a Rebel soldier burst through the smoke and ran at him. He had his head down as if looking for traps on the ground, his arms wrapped around his stomach. His gray uniform was stained red in a dozen places and as he came up on Crawford, he stopped. He stood, as if rooted to the ground, moved his arm from his belly and let his intestines spill out. He grinned at Crawford and then fell on his guts, dead.

Crawford stood there, bewildered. There were lines of sunlight bleeding through the haze of battle but he was in the eye of the storm. Nothing was happening around him. Just the roar of rifles, muskets, pistols and cannons. Just

the call of bugles and the shouting of men. But nothing that
he could see.

He stepped to the rear, saw two Union soldiers sitting
on the ground, back to back. He reached out to touch one
of them and noticed the bloody black hole in the side of his
head. A trickle of blood had flowed down the side of his
face and stained his uniform. His unseeing eyes were staring at the rifle he clutched in his bloodless fingers.

Crawford continued to move to the rear. He came out of
the haze and saw that the Union line had shifted again. He
was slightly in front of it. He ran to it and fell in with it,
but the Rebels seemed to have stopped. Slowly, he realized
that the sound of the battle had quieted. He could hear the
individual reports of the weapons now. He could hear the
shouted commands of the officers.

As he turned toward the summit of Little Round Top, he
saw Brown standing there, his rifle in his hand. Crawford,
still holding the captured flag ran up the hill and dropped to
the ground near Brown.

"How's it going, Colonel?"

"I've got the answer," Brown shouted at him. "I've got
the whole answer to this."

On the northern side of the Union perimeter, Kent and
Cunningham were crouched near the large stone structure
in the cemetery. Like most of the time travelers, and the
majority of the Union army, they had spent the day watching the maneuvering of the Rebels. Watching as the Rebels
had been riding to new positions, marching to new positions, moving in and out of Gettysburg, and even shooting
at the Union lines in front of them.

At noon, a sergeant came around, giving out orders for
the midday meal. Kent was taken off the line and told
to eat, while Cunningham had to stay were he was, guard-

ing the men who were eating. Kent slipped to the rear of
the formation, to where there were several huge cooking
fires, a line of white tents erected out of sight of the enemy
either in Gettysburg or along Seminary Ridge, and got into
line.

As he moved forward, he realized that he wasn't prepared to eat. He had no mess kit, or knife or fork. Brown,
when outfitting the men for the trip, hadn't thought that
any of that sort of thing would be necessary. Now, Kent
saw that it was. He slipped from the line and found the
head cook sitting on a log, smoking a huge cigar.

"Sergeant, I've lost my mess kit."

The man didn't seem to have heard. He chewed on the
cigar, switching it from one side of his mouth to the other.
Finally he looked up, blinked in the sunlight and said, "Not
my problem."

"I thought maybe you had some spares."

"You thought wrong. You lose your mess kit, you talk
to your supply sergeant or you go buy a new one."

Kent stood there looking at the man. He wore a white
coat over his uniform, but it was stained with food, grass
and dirt. There were yellowed stains under the arms and
ashes on the front.

After several seconds, Kent turned and walked between
two of the tents. As he approached the line again, he heard
a voice to the right.

"Let you borrie my kit for a half buck."

"What?" asked Kent.

"Let you borrie my kit for half a buck," repeated the
man. "I just washed it so it's clean."

"Yeah, Okay," said Kent. He dug in his pocket and
found a couple of coins. Collector's items where he came
from. He handed them over and took the kit. It wasn't that
he was so hungry that he had to eat, but more in the nature

of research. He wanted to taste the food that the Union army had to live on. To compare it with the food he remembered from Vietnam. Bad food that tasted as if it had been boiled for days and then fried. Food that didn't really resemble anything that he was familiar with. He just wondered if it was the same in the Union army.

When he got to the front of the line, the man serving dug a big, blackened spoon into a huge pot and dropped a baked potato into Kent's kit. He found another and put it by the first. Kent noticed that there were burnt spots on the skin.

He moved to the next position and was given a spoonful of beans. Not baked beans in a nice sauce, but black-eyed peas. He continued on, but there wasn't anything else given. He smiled as he walked across the bare earth and found a spot near a tree. He sat down, crossed his legs and picked up the potato. It was still warm. Kent ate it like it was an apple. He finished it and picked up the second, smaller one. He wished that he had some pepper and some butter for it, but found the taste intriguing. He wondered if there was some special way that the potatoes had been prepared.

With his spoon he ate the beans. They weren't as good as the potatoes but then, they were better than the majority of the meals he had eaten in Vietnam. When he finished, he washed the kit in a barrel of water that had been provided for that purpose and gave it back to the man who owned it.

"Thanks," said Kent.

"You need it tonight, you look me up and we'll work something out."

"Sure will."

Kent headed back to the line. He found Cunningham

sitting in the shade of the building, watching the front. Kent dropped to the ground beside him.

"Nice of you to return," said Cunningham.

"You going to eat?"

"No. I'm not that hungry for the food here. Besides, it's getting too late in the day."

Kent nodded and said, "I will say one thing though. The food is better than anything we got overseas."

"Well, I'm still not going to eat."

Kent nodded and sat back, leaning against the stone structure. He closed his eyes and let the impressions come to him. He could hear shooting somewhere along the lines, somewhere to the south, but didn't worry about it. He felt the hot breeze blowing that did nothing to dry the sweat on him. He patted at his forehead with the blue serge sleeve of his uniform jacket. He opened his eyes as there was a crash in front of him and saw a mushroom of smoke and dirt. A second later there was another and then another, and the men around him began to scramble for cover while two or three opened fire with their rifles.

Kent laughed at that, watching the men work feverishly to reload and waste another shot. Far in front, the Rebel soldiers under the command of Ewell waited as the cannonade became more intense. There were explosions all over the hill. A blossoming of dirt and debris that rained all around obscuring everything. Dozens of explosions, the cannon shells detonating among the Yankee troops. Some of them stood to flee. Others dived for the little protection available. Kent and Cunningham stayed where they were, knowing that they were safest if they didn't move.

Kent thought about the first mortar attack he had been in while in Vietnam. His first reaction had been to run. His second was to dive for the wall of his hootch, rolling close to it, figuring that the round would have to nearly hit him to hurt him. He had laid like that, listening to the explosions all over the camp, smelling the dank odor of freshly turned dirt and then the acrid stink of the burnt powder. He hadn't been worried, hadn't been scared until one of them hit close enough to rattle his teeth and nearly rupture his eardrums. He pressed his face to the dirt floor, inhaling the dust, his arms wrapped around his head. He had found himself praying.

But the next time, he had been casual about it. He had listened for the rounds, trying to determine if they were coming closer or moving away. He hadn't been scared. He had been annoyed because he had been shaken from a deep sleep.

Now he found the old feelings coming back. He watched the detonations of the Rebel cannon as the shells hit the hill almost randomly. He couldn't guess where the next one would fall. All he knew was that he didn't feel the fear of the first mortar attack. He watched with an almost detached interest.

Then, from behind him, came the booming of the Union artillery as they tried to destroy the Confederate cannon emplacements. The thing that he noticed most was the smoke. Each cannon shot blew clouds of it at the target. It hung in the air, over the field, oppressing everyone. It burned his lungs and stung his eyes. He found it hard to breathe. He had been lying on his stomach, but now he sat up, gulping at the air like a fish out of water.

He looked at Cunningham and said, "The Rebels aren't going to attack for a while. Let's get out of here."

"And do what?"

"Hell, who knows. Help out on Little Round Top where we can find some protection from their fucking artillery and some clean air to breathe."

"So that's it. You don't like breathing used air."

"And I don't like playing target."

There was an explosion close to them. Both flattened themselves and waited as the dirt cascaded onto their backs. A second detonation, closer, shook them. Kent turned his head as the last of the debris landed, and grinned at Cunningham.

"Now you want to get out of here?"

"Yeah. Now I want to get out of here. I want to get out real bad."

Kent looked around. Most of the men were crouching in the available cover, hiding. No one seemed to be paying attention to anyone else. Kent grabbed his rifle, got to his feet and hunched over. He ran to the south, away from the line, looking like a man trying to shield himself from rain. Cunningham was right behind him.

They moved through one brigade's area and as they crossed into another a burly sergeant stopped them. He stood in their path, his hands on his hips, and when they halted, he bellowed, over the sound of the cannons and the explosions, "Just where do you gentlemen think you are going?"

"Heading to our unit, Sergeant," said Kent.

"To your unit. And where are you coming from?"

Kent shot a glance at Cunningham and said, "Cemetery Hill. Our Colonel sent us over with a message for the brigadier there."

The sergeant looked them over carefully. He saw no signs that they were panicked soldiers. They were standing there, with the cannons booming around them, wanting to run in the direction of a battle. He could hear the heavy firing from rifles and muskets to the south. He looked over his shoulder and then back to Kent and Cunningham.

"All right, lads, I'll let you pass." He looked as if he was going to say more, but then just stepped to the side.

When they were out of earshot, Cunningham said, "Thought he was going to have us shot as deserters."

"Nah," said Kent. "We don't look like deserters. We look like soldiers on a mission for our Colonel."

"Running right into the middle of another battle."

"Yeah," said Kent. "Right into the middle. Maybe this isn't such a hot idea."

"I just hope that Brown and your friend Maddie have it all figured out so that we can punch out of here."

Kent stopped moving. "Figured out?" he said. And then realized what Cunningham meant. Had the change figured out so that they could get out of Gettysburg with history intact.

TWENTY-NINE

Cunningham and Kent found the majority of the mercenaries grouped near a large boulder on the northern side of Little Round Top. Yankee cannon were along the western edge, firing into the Rebel lines spread out east of the Emmitsburg Road, in the Peach Orchard and in the Devil's Den. The artillerymen were working together, loading, aiming and firing their weapons, keeping at it as one man ran between them, pouring water on the barrels. Clouds of smoke drifted across the summit of Little Round Top. Fires sprang up in front of the weapons that were quickly extinguished by the cannoneers.

Around them was a company of riflemen who were watching the ground around them, waiting for the Rebels. There was little talk, little jubilation in the Union lines. The men were grim and determined and scared. But none of them ran from their positions when the Rebel artillery began to shoot at them.

Kent took all this in and then dropped to the ground near Brown. He glanced at Maddie who looked at him with hooded eyes but said nothing.

Brown, on the other hand, did speak. "Tonight," he began, "we're going to have to abandon our position here. The Yankees seem to now understand the vulnerability of Little Round Top and won't let it be threatened again. According to Maddie, here, we have prevented the change that threw the Union army into a tailspin."

Pete Baily, who was covered with dirt, his face nearly black with it except for white circles around his eyes, grinned slowly and said, "That mean we're going to get out of here?"

"No," said Brown. "It means that there has been a change in history now. A change in the second history that put everything right. We have, at the very least, prevented the disaster that could have developed during the day." He shook his head, "But I don't think the danger is over."

"What's that mean," asked McGee.

"I have spotted the problem. I know why there was a change here at Gettysburg and it has nothing to do with a ripple effect. Has nothing to do with time adjusting to compensate for our appearance in 1836."

"Then we weren't responsible for the problem here," said McGee, underscoring Brown's meaning.

"That's right," said Brown. "At least not directly." He considered a dozen ways to tell them about it. Considered drawing it out. Then he just said, "It's Dennison."

"What?"

Brown looked at McGee. "The random factor in the equation is Dennison. I saw him. Saw him with the Rebels as they attacked the Peach Orchard."

Kent looked at Cunningham and then at Maddie. He

shrugged and said, "But that's impossible. He had no way to get here."

"That's where you're wrong," said Brown. "He couldn't travel here the way we did in just a few hours. He just stayed in 1836 and traveled to 1863 with the rest of the world. Let twenty-seven years pass."

"He waited twenty-seven years to get here?" said McGee.

"Yes," said Brown. "He looked to be forty-five or fifty. He wasn't in the front lines with the young men, but he was there on the attack. He's the reason there was a change here at Gettysburg."

"Then he could make changes elsewhere," said McGee.

"And that's the problem. I'm not sure where there will be another critical battle like this one. But if Dennison is able to tell the Rebels where the mistakes are made in other battles, he's liable to change the outcome of the war anyway. A setback here, yes. But that doesn't mean he won't be able to shift the war to the Rebels' advantage somewhere else. Get them to attack where the Union army is the weakest, causing the shift of men and material."

"So what do we do," said Baily. "I'm not thrilled with the idea of spending three years trying to guess where Dennison will show up."

"We end it here," said Brown. "Tonight."

"How?"

"Obviously we slip down and into the Rebel lines, looking for Dennison . . ."

"To do what?" asked McGee. "Kill him?"

"Shit no," said Brown. "We tell him what he's doing. Let him know that he's fouling up history. It's more than just a Rebel victory. It's a total defeat for the world."

"You think that'll make a difference," asked Kent.

"You don't know him," said Brown. "He'll understand. He was with us at the Alamo and understood there."

"He's not the man you knew," said Cunningham. "It's been twenty-seven years. What if he doesn't care about the world in the future? What if all he cares about is the Confederacy here and now."

"In that case," said Brown, "we kill him."

They spent an hour discussing how they were going to do it. Brown suggested two-man teams. They would work their way down the slopes of Little Round Top, find uniforms by taking them from the bodies of the dead and then circulate in the Rebel lines. There were so many men involved in the battle that each of them, by claiming to be a member of Pender's or Heth's divisions on the north side of the line, could probably pass. The men of McLaw's or Hood's divisions wouldn't be expected to know the men of the other divisions.

It wasn't long after sunset that they all slipped away from hiding on Little Round Top. To the north on Cemetery Hill, where Kent and Cunningham had been earlier in the day, there was heavy firing. By watching they could see flashes in the clouds of smoke that hung close to the ground like a fog. The whole thing looked and sounded like a thunderstorm sitting on the hill.

As Brown had suggested, they split into groups of two as they reached the foot of the hill. Brown and Pete Baily turned slightly to the north and worked their way past an outcropping of rock, into a thin stand of trees. They found a group of Union soldiers sitting there, one of them watching to the west, searching for the Rebels while the others sat hunched near a miniature fire waiting for the coffee to brew.

Neither Brown nor Baily said anything to the men. They

just looked at them, dark shapes in a flickering light, and then slipped through the trees. On the open ground, Brown crouched, letting his eyes adjust to the darkness until he could see the black shapes of the dead men scattered around. The wounded had been collected earlier, in an uneasy truce that wasn't really called by either side. The medical men, the doctors, their assistants, the nurses, and the corpsmen, moved over the field picking up the injured.

Crouching low, sometimes crawling forward on hands and knees, or on his belly, Brown wormed his way across the open area. He passed a dozen dead men, stopping long enough to examine their uniforms. The majority of them were Yankees. The uniforms of the Rebels were so bloody and damaged that it was obvious that the owners had died. It was true that some blood could be explained as that from an enemy soldier killed in a hand-to-hand fight, but the massive amounts on the coats he saw defied explanation.

They crossed a thin creek that drained into Plum Run. On the western side of it, they came to the Peach Orchard. It was strangely quiet now that the battle for it had ended. Brown halted at the edge of the trees and looked into it, letting the hazy moonlight illuminate the ground. Black shadows danced in patterns over the ground created by the breeze and trees. Lumps on the ground that were the bodies of the dead. And almost no noise from the Peach Orchard, as if it was a graveyard.

In the north, there was shooting. Cannons and rifles, as the two armies still fought. But in the south, in the Peach Orchard it was as quiet as death.

Brown looked over his shoulder at Baily who was kneeling by the trunk of a peach tree. Brown shrugged and stood up, moving deeper into the Peach Orchard. Before he had taken more than three steps, he came to the first body, a Rebel soldier missing an arm and most of his head.

Spread out as far as he could see were more bodies. Dozens of them. Hundreds of them.

And all around them was equipment. Rifles, bayonets, knives, field kits and mess kits, boots lying by themselves, coats and shirts. Anything needed for an army could be found on the field, lying next to bodies, or on them, or under them.

Brown discovered a dead soldier with a uniform coat in perfect condition. The man had lost both legs at the knee and it looked as if he had tried to put a tourniquet on one while he bled to death through the other. There was a sticky pool of blood at the ends of his legs but none of it had gotten onto his coat. Brown stripped the man, and tossed his own blue tunic on the ground.

As he put on the coat, he caught a strong whiff of copper from the pool of blood. It was the one thing that remained the same in all battlefields throughout history. There might be other odors. Horses or gunpowder or diesel fuel, but the one constant was the smell of blood. A thick, coppery smell that Brown equated with death. Gallons of spilled blood that made the ground slippery with mud and filled the air with copper.

Brown felt a hand on his shoulder and turned to find Baily. "Think we better get moving, Colonel."

Brown nodded and stepped over the dead man and onto the hand of another. He twisted his ankle and fell to one knee. He grinned up at Baily, but it was a grin with little mirth in it. He pointed toward the north, to the edge of the Peach Orchard.

"Let's head in that direction," he said.

"Yes sir."

As they approached the edge of the trees, Baily whispered, "You see a hole in my coat?"

Brown examined it and said, "No. Looks like a stain

near the shoulder." He looked again and said, "You shouldn't have picked a sergeant's coat."

"Why not?"

"There are fewer sergeants than privates."

"I don't think it matters," said Baily.

"You're probably right," said Brown. He turned and nearly tripped over another body. He crouched and stared at the face and then moved carefully to the Emmitsburg Road. He stopped, kneeling in the ditch alongside of it, searching the ground on the other side, looking for the enemy.

"What is it now?"

"I think we made our way into the Rebel lines."

"Great," said Baily sounding as if it was anything but great. "Now what?"

"It would seem to me," said Brown, "that Dennison would be hanging around the Rebel headquarters. We'll see how close we can get to one and watch to see if he appears."

Cunningham and Kent worked their way from one outcropping of rock to the next, running between them like soldiers in a war movie. They stopped as they reached the bottom of a hill, where there were bodies of nearly a thousand dead men spread out in front of them. They stayed there for a moment, surveying the field, seeing shadows flitting across it as the medical men searched for badly wounded men who might have been missed in the first sweep.

Cunningham watched the process and then stepped out, grabbing a dead man under the arms. He nodded at Kent and said, "Help me."

"That man's dead," said Kent quietly.

"So what? He makes the perfect cover. We're carrying a

wounded man to a field hospital. No one's going to shoot at us. No one's going to challenge us."

Kent stepped forward and took the man under the knees, lifting. For some reason the dead man seemed heavier than a living one would have. Idly, he wondered if that was where the term *deadweight* came from and then put the thought out of his mind.

"We've still got to get Confederate uniforms," said Kent.

"We can worry about that once we get clear of this field. They'll be plenty of opportunities."

They carefully made their way across the field, avoiding the black lumps that were the bodies of the soldiers killed during the afternoon. No one challenged them. No one stopped them. In fact there were others moving around the field, searching for friends who were missing, or caring for the wounded.

They reached a clump of trees and set the body down next to the trunk of a large elm. Kent felt strange about that, as if abandoning a friend. He knew the thought was irrational, but he couldn't help it. It was as if the man had protected them as they crossed the battlefield.

The thoughts were interrupted when Cunningham loomed out of the dark next to him and said, "I've found my uniform." He glanced at Kent and asked, "What in the hell are you doing?"

Kent shrugged and realized that Cunningham probably hadn't seen the gesture. "Saying thanks to a friend, I guess."

"Friend? The guy's dead."

"Never mind," said Kent. "I don't think I could explain it to you. I'm not sure that I understand it myself."

"Fine. You want to grab a uniform so we can get this show on the road?"

Kent turned and checked a couple of bodies. Two of them were Union soldiers. The first Rebel he found had lost an arm and then taken a round in the chest. The whole front of this uniform was a sticky mess. Kent stared at it for a moment and saw it shift in the pale moonlight. He reached out and then jumped back as a buzzing assaulted him and he realized that the soldier's chest was covered with insects.

He moved on quickly, found a man lying face down. He rolled him over and saw that his uniform was in good shape. He worked the man out of it and then took off his own. He dropped it and then said, "Hey, Bob, our uniform's are bullet-resistant. We can't just throw them away."

"Can't carry them either," said Cunningham. "You make a lousy spy if you enter the enemy's camp carrying the uniform of the enemy."

"Custer used to wear the uniform he captured from a Rebel general."

"Custer had two things working form him. One, he too, was a general and two, he was with people who knew him. We're running around in the dark, among soldiers who don't know who the fuck we are. Besides, with a couple of thousand dead Yankees lying around, who's going to steal a uniform? You want a souvenir, all you got to do is take a short walk."

Kent shrugged. He tossed his coat on the ground and then picked it up again. He hung it on a low branch in a tree, hoping that he would be able to find it later. That finished, he said, "Let's go find Dennison."

"You know we have about two chances to find him. Zero and none."

"Oh, I don't know," said Kent. "I think if we circulate

enough we're bound to run into him. See him in the distance or something."

"Yeah," said Cunningham. "I believe that." He didn't speak again as he reached the Emmitsburg Road. He was sure that they had passed the edge of the Rebel lines and were in fact behind them. He shook his head, thinking that it was a pretty loose line that allowed men to walk through it without being challenged, and then realized that two men did not an attack make. The Rebels were probably more concerned with the movements of the Union soldiers on Cemetery Ridge.

They came to a large camp, maybe two hundred soldiers on a thin line. They were challenged by a sentry and gave the cover story that Brown had suggested during the briefing. The Rebel corporal told them to advance and then told them to pass when he saw the color of their uniforms. Kent detoured toward the camp, saw the faces of some of the soldiers, but didn't see anyone who looked like Dennison.

When they were out of earshot of the guard, Kent said, "We've got to do something to speed this up."

"What do you suggest?"

"That we're looking for a friend of ours who got separated from our unit. Tell the guards that we're looking for a man who's about fifty, who was riding a horse and who seems to have the ear of some of the generals. How many guys like that can there be?"

Cunningham stopped walking and rubbed his chin. "Given the fact that our guy is not a general himself, or a high ranking officer, probably not too many. Shit, it just might work."

"And it means that we don't have to search everywhere. We can ask around and maybe someone will point us in the right direction."

They continued on, looping through the woods on the

west side of the Emmitsburg Road. It took them twenty minutes to find another Rebel outpost. Again they were halted by the guard, challenged and then told, "Come forward to be recognized."

Cunningham stepped close while Kent remained a couple of paces behind him. Cunningham said, "We're looking for a friend of ours. Older gentleman, might have been riding with the general."

The guard shook his head and spit a foul-smelling stream of tobacco juice. "Nope," he said, "don't sound familiar, but then I don't confer with the General all that much."

"Seen anyone like that. Maybe riding with a staff officer. I think he would have been wearing civilian clothes."

"Wearin' civilian clothes?" said the guard.

"Could have been."

"Ya'all don't seem to know much about this friend of yours."

"Haven't seen him since this morning," said Cunningham, "and a lot has happened today."

"That's true. No, I haven't seen anyone like that."

"Well, thanks," said Cunningham. "We'll be going."

"Ya'all be careful out in them woods. Lotsa Yanks still running around even after the whooping we gave 'em today."

"We'll be mighty careful," said Cunningham.

They ducked back into the trees, now moving north toward the area where Brown and Baily were supposed to be. After only ten or fifteen minutes, they spotted a flickering through the trees that could only mean a fire. It didn't necessarily mean there were men near it. The shooting during the day had started dozens of small grass fires that the soldiers had to put out before they developed into a large-scale conflagration.

But, as they approached, they were challenged. This time Kent went forward and asked the questions. The guard, a tall, thin man who was holding his rifle at port arms said, "General McLaw was with someone like that this afternoon. Seen it myself."

"McLaw," repeated Kent. "His headquarters are . . ."

"Over yonder. In the trees there. Meybe a mile or two from here. Meybe less."

"Hey, thanks," said Kent.

"Where ya'all from?" asked the guard, suddenly suspicious. "Ya'all don't sound like ya'all are from down home."

"Missouri," said Kent quickly. "Rode all the way from Missouri to get into this fight and then got separated from our friend."

"Must be an important friend if he goes riding with the General."

"Important enough," said Kent, backing up. He saw Cunningham out of the corner of his eye and spun. Quickly, they disappeared into the woods.

When they were away from the guard, Cunningham said, "Now what?"

"We try to find General McLaw's headquarters."

"And do what? What are we going to tell the guards if they want to know why we're searching for the General."

"Simple enough," said Kent. "We'll tell them we have a message for the General from Early or Ewell. That he is supposed to support their attacks in the morning by harassing the Union line. It'll sound convincing if anyone asks and give us a chance to snoop around."

"I don't know, Andy," said Cunningham. "Remember in basic training they told us never to lie to captors because the story you make up might somehow compromise a real plan."

"Jesus, Bob, we know what happens tomorrow. Ewell isn't going to attack. Pickett is. We're not giving anyone ideas. We're just covering our butts."

From somewhere in the trees they heard a bark of laughter and then sudden silence. They realized that they had come to another company's area and that there would be guards around.

"You going to go along with this?" whispered Kent.

"Of course," said Cunningham quietly. "Don't have a whole lot of choice on the matter."

"Okay. You let me do the talking again."

They went through the challenge routine and then Kent said, "I have a message for General McLaw from General Ewell. I need escort to his headquarters."

The guard, who still hadn't come out of the shadows, yelled, "Sergeant of the Guard, post number seven."

They stood waiting until a Rebel sergeant who looked like a mountain moving through trees appeared. He stared at Kent and Cunningham and asked, "Ya'all want?"

"Need to find General McLaw with a message from General Ewell."

The sergeant moved close, studied them, looking at their coats and then their boots. "Ya'all wearing Yankee boots."

"Lots of us are wearing Yankee boots tonight."

The sergeant laughed and said, "Guess so. Ya'all follow me and don't get lost or ya'all be picking lead out of y'all's hides."

Kent and Cunningham fell in behind the sergeant. He wound his way through the trees, coming out in a small clearing. He stopped at the edge and pointed to a slight rise about two hundred yards away. "General McLaw is over there now. Ya'all can find him there."

"Thanks," said Kent. He started off across the open area

with Cunningham right behind him. They passed a couple of groups of soldiers, found a pathway and followed it until they came to a line of trees. They walked through it and found a group of tents. There were a couple of lanterns hanging from the poles on the tents, forty or fifty soldiers posted around the perimeter, and a dozen officers. Standing in the middle of the group, pointing at a map that had been tacked on a board, was the man they were looking for. Steven Dennison was briefing the Rebel officers on the placement of the Union troops, readying the Confederates for the fighting the next day.

THIRTY

As soon as they spotted Dennison, they stopped moving. Kent crouched, one knee on the soft earth, his rifle at the ready. Cunningham stood beside him, watching Dennison as he talked to an officer near the main tent.

"Now what?" whispered Cunningham.

"We can't go get Brown," responded Kent. "Not enough time. We've got to handle this ourselves."

"So what do we do?" asked Cunningham.

Kent rubbed a hand over his face, feeling the stubble of his beard, the dirt from the battle, and sweat from the lingering heat of the day. He wiped his hand on his coat and said, "Talk to him. Just talk to him. Get him away from here and tell him what he's done."

"That won't work," said Cunningham.

"Okay," snapped Kent. "You want to shoot him now? Surrounded by the entire Army of Virginia? Go right ahead."

"That's not what I meant."

"Fine. Tell me what you meant then."

Cunningham stared at the ground and then back up at Dennison who held the reins of a horse in one hand. The Rebel officer had taken a step to the rear but they were still engaged in conversation.

"We better do something fast," said Cunningham.

Kent stood and began walking forward. He burst from the circle of shadow that surrounded the campsite and move rapidly forward. There was a shout to his right as a guard saw him, but Kent didn't stop. He approached the two men and when they looked at him, Kent felt his throat constrict, making speech impossible.

The officer moved toward him and demanded, "What is your business here, private?"

Kent glanced to the rear, but Cunningham hadn't moved. He turned and said to the officer, "Have some information for, ah, Mr. Dennison, here."

"You have the wrong man," said the officer. "This is Mr. Harrison. He doesn't have time to waste with the likes of you."

Now Dennison stepped forward and put a hand on the officer's sleeve. "It's all right, Lieutenant, I know this man. Andy Kent, isn't it?"

"Yes sir, it is, Mr. Harrison."

"What can I do for you?" asked Dennison.

Kent hitchhiked a thumb over his shoulder, toward Cunningham and said, "We need to talk with you for a few minutes. That's all."

"It's all right, Lieutenant," said Dennison, repeating himself. "I will see General Longstreet in a few minutes. Thank you for your help."

"If you're sure, sir," said the Lieutenant. He touched the

brim of his cap with two of his fingers in a half salute and added, "If you'll excuse me."

When the Lieutenant was out of sight, Dennison grabbed Kent at the elbow, nearly dragging him across the open ground. "What the fuck are you doing here?" he hissed.

Kent stopped moving and spun on Dennison. "I could ask you the same thing."

"You're going to spoil everything," Dennison shot back. "Don't you realize that?"

Cunningham moved in and stood in front of Dennison as Kent said, "You're already spoiling history. You have no idea of the trouble you've caused in the future. A future that you wouldn't recognize it's so different."

Dennison jerked around, almost as if to free himself from Kent. "All I've done is provide some information about Union troop movements to the Confederate forces. I told them to take Little Round Top." He smiled. "They almost made it."

"I've got news for you," said Cunningham. "In the future we've just seen, they did take it and the whole Union defense collapsed. We were forced to intervene."

"What?" said Dennison, his voice rising to a high-pitched shriek. "You did what?"

Now Kent took his elbow and directed him toward the trees, away from the Rebel camp and the Rebel guards. As they moved into the darkness, Kent said, "We had to put everything back. You've got to come with us."

Dennison shook himself free and said, "I've got to report to General Longstreet and General Lee and stop the attack tomorrow. That's what I've got to do."

"No!" said Cunningham. "You can't just flit through time making changes where it suits you. The damage to the future is unbelievable."

"I don't give a shit about the future," said Dennison, the hysteria rising in his voice again. "I'm only concerned with the here and now. You have no right to be here. No right at all."

"Look," said Kent reasonably. "Why don't you just come with us and talk to Colonel Brown. Let him explain it to you and then you'll understand."

"I understand everything that I have to. You are here to sabotage the South. You're here to help the Union win so that the South will be crushed and ruined."

"We're only here to make sure that history follows the right path," said Cunningham.

"The path that you say is right. Well I say that the path I want is the right one and you can't stop me. I'm not going to talk to Brown because he won't understand this anymore than you do. You and your prejudices about how the future is supposed to be. A bright future built on the destruction of the South."

"That's not true," said Kent lowering his voice. "All we're trying to do is make sure that history is preserved the way it is supposed to be."

"How do you know what it's supposed to be," demanded Dennison. "I'll bet in the future there are books that show the great Confederate victory at Gettysburg."

"You know how it's supposed to be," said Cunningham. "If the South was supposed to win, you wouldn't have to be here making changes. Now, please, Steven, come with us. Talk to Brown."

"No," said Dennison, moving away from them. "I will not. You've got to get out of here. Now." He reached for the holster strapped around his waist.

Kent took a step to the rear and unconsciously pulled back the hammer of his rifle. "Be reasonable," he said.

"Don't!" shouted Cunningham. "Let's talk this through.

You know us. We're reasonable men." He eased to the side, swinging his rifle out to cover Dennison.

"Time for talk is over," said Dennison, his voice sad. "Time for talk is over." He unsnapped the flap and was reaching around to grab the butt of the pistol.

"Think about it," said Kent. "Talk to us. Come on."

"It's too late for talk."

"It's never too late," said Cunningham.

Dennison drew his weapon and as it cleared the holster, he fired. There was a bright flare of light that stabbed into the night. The bullet buried itself in the ground near Kent's feet.

Kent dived to the right and rolled as Dennison fired again, the strobelike effect freezing the action.

Cunningham swung his rifle up and fired from the hip. He saw the flame from the muzzle, nearly four feet long, reach out and touch Dennison on the side. He heard the wet smack of the round striking flesh and heard Dennison grunt in surprise and pain.

But Dennison didn't fall. He grabbed his side with his free hand, doubled over to the left, trying to thumb back the hammer for a third shot.

Kent was on the move then. He got to his knees, aimed and fired. The round stuck Dennison in the chest, throwing him back to the ground. As he hit, Cunningham moved in and thrust his bayonet into Dennison's throat.

"What the fuck did you do that for?"

"Make sure," said Cunningham. "If he's not dead, he can still make trouble."

Then, suddenly there was a shout from the Rebel camp and they could hear men crashing into the woods after them. For an instant, Kent considered standing his ground and telling the Rebels that they had been ambushed by Yankee soldiers, but realized the story wouldn't stand up.

"Let's scram," he said and plunged into the trees. Cunningham was right behind him.

There was a shout on the left that was answered by someone behind them. Kent slid to a stop, saw a flickering of movement and yelled, "This way. I saw someone running this way."

Cunningham grinned at Kent, his teeth flashing and said, "Brilliant idea."

"Thought so too."

They slowed slightly, letting the Rebel soldiers get closer. Cunningham pointed and yelled at them, "Through there. They went through there."

The Rebel line spread out and entered into a thicker part of the forest as Kent and Cunningham diverted to the south. A Rebel sergeant yelled at them but then turned to follow his men as they plunged into the treeline.

As they got away from the Rebel searchers, they slowed down. Again they found Rebel companies and were challenged by the pickets. Since they were coming from the other direction, from the Rebel's strength, the guards passed them quickly and easily. No one seemed concerned about the shooting because there were shots being fired all over Seminary Ridge and Cemetery Ridge. There were snipers and skirmishers posted in the no-man's-land between the two armies so that, just as the night before, there was always firing somewhere by someone.

Crossing the Emmitsburg Road was a little trickier than it had been, but they made it by hugging the ground and then dodging into the Peach Orchard. Once in there, they tossed away the Rebel uniform coats they had taken and then scrambled to the rear. They weren't challenged by a Union picket until they were at the base of Little Round Top and since they knew who held it, knew General War-

ren's name and the units of his makeshift brigade, they
were taken to the summit.

They moved among the cannon emplacements and the
rifle pits until they were on the eastern side of Little Round
Top. They found Maddie and a couple of the others sitting
in the shelter of several gigantic rocks, a fire laid against
the base of one so that the glow would be hidden from the
Rebels.

When Maddie saw Kent, she leaped up and threw her
arms around him, mumbling into his ear. Kent pulled back,
looked at her and then to the others and said, "It's over."

Brown and Baily came out of the gloom and Brown
asked, "What'd you say?"

"It's over, colonel. We found Dennison . . ."

"Where? What was he doing?"

"Over near McLaw's headquarters talking to a lieutenant. We had to kill him," said Cunningham.

"Had to?" said Brown. "I thought talking to him would
be enough."

"We had a chance to talk to him. I think he was slightly
crazy," said Kent. "Wanted the South to rise again and this
was the opportunity. We tried to reason with him, but he
pulled his pistol . . ."

"Still," said Brown.

"Hell, Colonel," said Cunningham. "We even gave him
the first shot. He fired three times and he wasn't trying to
scare us off. He was trying to kill us."

Brown moved forward so that he was inside the glow of
the fire. He crouched and picked at a stick. "Damn," he
said. "Just damn it all anyway."

"Nothing we could do," repeated Kent.

"I don't doubt it," said Brown. "Don't doubt it at all."

"We can punch out now," said Maddie. "We don't have
to wait because there won't be anymore changes."

"That may not be true. We don't know what Dennison was telling that Lieutenant," said Brown.

"I don't think it makes any difference," said Kent. "I don't think there is anything that Dennison could have told them that would make any difference this late in the battle. There aren't any weaknesses left to exploit."

"That's not necessarily true," said Brown, "but it would be harder to find something than it was today." He looked up and said, "Our reports showed that the major changes were made on the second day and we stopped those, but now that things have changed, Dennison could have had something else in mind."

"So what do we do?" asked Kent.

"Wait here for morning to see if there is anything that sticks out as being significant. Watch for Pickett's Charge and see if it succeeds instead of fails."

"That leaves us in here, for what, another twelve hours?" asked Cunningham.

"Depending on the time now, yes, twelve, fourteen hours. Something like that."

"What do we do?" asked Maddie. "We have to be careful because of the possible effects our presence will have on the future."

"All I'm suggesting," said Brown, "is that we stay and watch the attacks tomorrow. I'm not suggesting that we get down there in the fight. I'm not suggesting that we tell Meade or anyone else about Pickett's Charge. I'm only saying that we determine that history, at least here, is on the right path."

"We can check that out when we get back," said Maddie. "Just pick up a history book."

"But if we're here," said Brown, "on the scene, so to speak, we can fix it right away and not have to fuck around in the future."

Maddie looked at the others and said, "I suppose if we just watch, there shouldn't be any trouble."

"It's one of the great events in history," said Kent. "People know the North won, and they know Lee was here, but about the only other name anyone can remember from Gettysburg is Pickett."

"Then it's settled," said Brown. "We watch tomorrow's activities and if there is no change, we slip home and everyone is happy."

THIRTY-ONE

The day dawned hot and hazy. To the north along Culp's Hill, the fighting continued, the Union soldiers attacking Rebel positions to drive them back toward Gettysburg. The firing there began about the time the sun came up and had been increasing ever since. Cannon had joined the battle and from Little Round Top the mercenaries could only see the flashes of the explosions and the clouds of dust thrown up by them. The smoke created by the firing of the cannons added to the haze until nearly all of Culp's Hill was lost to sight.

Brown climbed down from the rock where he had stood watching the battle progress and said, "It looks like it's going according to history. The Union is in full possession of the hill."

"Then we can punch out," said Kent.

"No." insisted Brown. "We have to watch the final hand played out. We have to be sure."

220

They moved to the rear of the hill and watched the shifting of the Union lines. There were now several Union regiments on the summits of both Little Round Top and Big Round Top. Artillery had been brought up too. The Union flank was secured, but Brown knew the problem was going to be the center of the line. He wondered if he should ride over to Meade's headquarters and tell him that he suspected a Rebel attack to the center of the line, but as he watched, more Union troops began to fill in there. Meade was waiting for the Rebels too.

Brown and his tiny force settled down on the eastern side of Little Round Top where they were invisible to the Rebels and had a big breakfast. They took their time eating, knowing that the real push would not begin for several hours.

They listened to firing in the north. A rattling of air, a crash of thunder and flashes of lightning, all man-made. The ground seemed to tremble with the sounds of the battle to the north and then it stopped, almost as if someone had commanded it. A silence that was nearly deafening.

Brown leaped to his feet and ran to the forward edge of Little Round Top, but there was nothing below him except more Union soldiers. He used McGee's binoculars, but Pickett and his generals had concealed their soldiers well. He could see no movement in the woods at the foot of Seminary Ridge. He could see nothing that betrayed the Confederate battle plan.

He spent the rest of the morning watching. Union soldiers on the front lines were throwing up breastworks of stone and dirt, trying to create barriers that would turn the Rebel assault and stop Rebel bullets.

And then he saw some of the Union soldiers drop away from the front, moving to the rear to sit in the shade of the trees or fences or anything else they could find. Brown knew that the time was getting close.

At that moment it seemed that the battlefield had sprouted volcanoes. The ground rumbled and shook and the air was split with a roar that continued to build. Brown saw the smoke boiling down Seminary Ridge as the Rebel artillery began to fire. He turned in time to see some of the rounds land among the Union lines, destroying the fences, the weapons, and killing the men who waited for the assault.

The cannons on Little Round Top responded, but it didn't bother the Confederates. They threw more into the cannonade, so that it sounded like the longest, loudest peal of thunder ever heard. The detonations spotted the ground on Cemetery Ridge destroying everything around it and filling the air with shrapnel that stripped the bark and leaves from trees and bushes.

For what seemed like a long time, the Union cannon remained silent, the infantry absorbing the brunt of the Rebel fire. Then, slowly, the Union batteries began to reply, raining shot and shell down on the Rebel positions, firing at the enemy batteries and troops.

Brown watched the show quietly. He saw men break from the Union ranks, fleeing to the top of Cemetery Ridge to disappear on the eastern slope. He saw others slowly slip down the hill to take up positions behind any cover available. He saw Union batteries, under heavy fire, explode. He saw cannons, caissons and ammunition destroyed and he saw men die.

Then, suddenly, at the height of the counter-battery duel, the Union cannon fell silent. There was maneuvering on Cemetery Ridge as some of the cannon seemed to withdraw.

Brown spun so that he was looking at the trees on Seminary Ridge, watching them closely as a long, gray line appeared, moving slowly and quietly toward the Union soldiers.

The lines kept coming and the Union artillery began firing again, ripping huge holes in the lines. Dozens of Rebels fell, but they didn't run. They didn't waver. They marched straight ahead, keeping quiet, not firing.

The men on Little Round Top and the positions on the flank of the Rebel assault began to shoot, unable to miss because of the mass of men. Thousands of them moving more rapidly now, trying to cover the open ground in front of them.

Then, on the far north, one of the Rebel regiments was hit by a wild burst of fire from a Yankee regiment. It proved to be too much for them and they broke, fleeing for cover. But that was the only unit to act that way. The rest of the Rebels continued the advance, moving ever faster.

It seemed that the ground exploded. The fire and flame from the cannon, the clouds of smoke and dust, hid the Rebels from the Yankee gunners and it would seem that no one could survive in the deathtrap. But the Confederate soldiers kept moving, kept coming.

Then all at once there was a cry from the Rebel lines and they began a surging charge across the remainder of the open ground. The firing from the Union positions was sporadic at best because the range was too far for their rifles and muskets.

The three attacking divisions seemed to merge then, rushing forward, guiding on the clump of trees in the center of the Union lines. The firing increased slowly. More of the attackers fell. There was a volley as a Union brigade opened fire at a Rebel regiment only two hundred yards away. Hundreds died in the space of seconds. They were engulfed in a cloud of smoke and fire. Bits of bodies were tossed in the air. Equipment flew apart. But the Rebels who survived came on, into the wall of lead that chopped them up.

There was a rising shout from all the Rebel lines and they hit the front of the Union then. There was an audible crash as the two forces were mixed and the fighting became hand-to-hand. There was shouting and screaming heard over the crash of the cannon and the din of the rifles. There were bugles and orders. Horses screaming in fear and pain. The sound swelled and swelled until it was impossible to hear anything at all.

The smoke from burnt gunpowder boiled around the battling men hiding them and then revealing them. It blotted out the sun and created a world of twilight where the men were only ghostly shapes locked in combat. On a personal level, it was one man against another. Bayonet against bayonet in a foggy landscape that looked as if it had been moved from the Earth to another planet.

And in that cloud, men died. Some quickly, a bullet in the head or in the heart. Some of them disappeared in the detonation of cannon shells. Others lost limbs and bled to death quickly, their blood mingling with that of hundreds, thousands of others and turning the ground into a bloody quagmire.

The Rebel lines surged forward in a final effort to overrun the Union positions. Some of the Rebels managed to climb the fence that marked the line. They gained the batteries, overrunning them. They reached toward the house that was Meade's headquarters, shouting in their victory. Shouting as they tried to cut the Union line in two.

At the angle where Pickett's and Pettigrew's divisions met, the Union counterattacked. More Yankee troops thrown into the battle, trying to swing the outcome. Thousands of fresh troops wading in with bayonet, sword and pistol, driving at the heart of the Confederate attack. Troops firing from the Angle poured a devastating fire into the Confederates, killing hundreds of them.

General Garnet tried to rally his men. With his hat on the point of his sword, he rushed forward, to lead his men, urging them onward. He rode through the melee, shouting and commanding, only to disappear in a cloud of smoke. Moments later his riderless horse, covered with blood, reappeared.

Other Rebels shouted and leaped a low stone wall, rushing a disorganized Pennsylvania infantry regiment that fled in fright. But there was another Pennsylvania unit waiting and they opened fire, stopping the Rebel advance. In moments every Confederate soldier who had crossed the wall was either dead, wounded or captured.

That signaled the end of the Rebel success. All around the same thing was happening. Rebel soldiers were dying too quickly. Others were turning from the wall of fire and steel that was being thrown at them. The chain of command was disintegrating as Rebel officer after Rebel officer died trying to rally the men.

There was never any command to retreat. The Rebels seemed to realize that they couldn't take the Union positions. There were too many Yankees there, who were too well armed and too well trained. They had not fled under the cannonade and had not fled when the armies crashed together. They had held their ground, fighting for their lives until the ground under them was red with their blood.

Slowly the Rebel lines began to retreat. They withdrew from the Angle and the stone walls on the slopes of Cemetery Ridge. First only a few men fighting their way to the rear and then more of them until the tide had been turned.

Now they had to endure the Union rifle fire and artillery as they re-crossed the open ground. This time, their goal was the safety of Seminary Ridge, where their fellows waited. The Yankees continued to pour a devastating fire into them. Hundreds who had survived the assault, died during the retreat.

Union officers, many of whom were wounded, tried to rally their men. Tried to force them into an attack on the Rebels, but the men had seen too much. Too many had died. Too many had been wounded. And there was too much blood on the ground. They were bone-weary, sickened men who wanted nothing more of the glory of battle. They only wanted the opportunity to survive, and to go home to tell of the horror they had seen.

In an hour and a half, it was over. Thousands of men had lost their lives in the fight. Many thousands more were wounded. But when the smoke and dust cleared, it was the tired, sweaty men of the Union who had won the day.

Brown sat on one of the rocks of Little Round Top, holding his borrowed binoculars in both hands. The blood had drained from his face as he watched the battle. Watched the butchery of the men of both armies. Even after the two sides had separated and firing had died away, Brown sat there, staring. He had never seen anything like it. Never in all his years of fighting had he seen anything like the assault by Pickett. It was an incredible attack that had turned into a bloodbath.

Finally, he got to his feet and walked over to where Maddie sat, her eyes to the south, away from the battle. He touched her shoulder and in a husky voice said, "History has been written. We can get out of here any time you want."

She looked up at him and said, "What about Custer?"

"History is on the right course now. This battle is over and Custer will have survived." He dropped to the ground, the stink of burnt powder filling the air, the cries of the wounded haunting the fields.

"It's finally over," was all he could say.

THIRTY-TWO

David Jackson sat in his office. A spacious place with four windows that looked out on a green, tree-studded park. Along one wall was a series of floor-to-ceiling bookcases that held hundreds of history volumes. Books that he had moved through the past to buy, cross-checking the historical references to make sure that no changes had been inadvertently introduced. On the left side of his massive desk was a computer keyed into the mainframe housed in the basement of the building. It too held history records, as well as the complete design program for the Tucker Transfer.

On the wall opposite him was a map of the United States, including Alaska and Hawaii, showing the locations of historical events. There were flags for the battlefields of the Revolutionary War and the Civil War. Flags marking the fights with the Plains Indians including the Custer Massacre. Flags for the locations of the development of the atomic bomb such as Oak Ridge and Chicago and Alamogordo. Flags marking the race riots of the 1960s and flags for the scenes of major crimes. It was a crowded map that showed Jackson a diversity of historical events of the fifty United States.

There was a buzz from the right side of his desk and he punched the button next to a flashing light. The tiny viewscreen brighted and he saw the face of one of his assistants. "We've a retrieval call," she said.

Jackson looked to the right wall, where the chart of activities hung. He noticed that there were no field teams out and therefore none that should want to be recalled. He leaned close to the microphone and said, "I'll be right down."

Jackson left his office, walked along the carpeted hallway and stopped in front of the elevator. He touched the button and then turned, looking back at the walls. They were lined with color photographs of historical events. Photos from the Roman Empire, the building of the Pyramids, photos of the short, stooped ancestors of the human race as they foraged across the plains of Africa millions of years ago. Photos of Washington's farewell speech and the signing of the Declaration of Independence.

There was a quiet ding behind him and the elevator doors whispered open. Jackson got in and headed for the basement. Once there, he walked down another brightly lighted hallway that was lined with more photos. He stopped near a brown door that had a red light recessed above it. The light was out, so Jackson opened the door.

Inside was the control room for the shoots. There were three positions for the technicians and one for the supervisor. Two of the positions were occupied. Jackson slipped into the supervisor's chair and said, "All right, Sarah, what have you got."

"Recall transmitted from 1863. Spacio coordinates suggest the recall comes from southern Pennsylvania."

Jackson spun in his chair and pulled the computer keyboard closer and typed a series of numbers and then watched as the display paraded across the screen in a bright green pattern. He studied it for a moment and then asked, "Any possibility of a malfunction of the equipment?"

"Cross-checked twice. Nothing at this end," said Sarah. "If we had a field team out, I'd suggest that we recall it assuming that we don't have an error in the receiver."

Jackson shook his head. "What are the possibilities that we're getting a recall from a team that we haven't sent yet?"

Sarah shrugged and ran a quick check on her computer keyboard. "There is always that possibility, but it hasn't happened before."

"And if it is a team we haven't sent yet, somewhere in the future we'll recall them anyway and this incident can be marked closed."

"There is another possibility," said Sarah. She had been facing the console, her eyes locked on the receiver, watching the coding on it. She turned and faced Jackson. "It could be a team sent into the past that inadvertantly made a change that created a new history. Wiped out the record of their departure. Now they want to come home and we don't know about them because of the change."

Jackson tugged at his ear as he thought about it. Sarah's point was well taken. But then there were a dozen other possibilities. Some kind of trick for some unknown reason, a malfunction, an electrical disturbance, someone trying to penetrate their organization from outside, not only outside the United States but outside their own time.

"Do we retrieve them?" asked Sarah.

Jackson let his eyes fall to the floor. There were too

many unpredictable elements in this. He turned so that he could scan the board. He didn't like anything about this and knew that he would have to say something because it was a problem that wouldn't just go away.

"I can't see a situation developing where we wouldn't know we have people in the past. We'll continue to monitor, but take no action."

THE ETERNAL MERCENARY
By Barry Sadler

_Casca #1: **THE ETERNAL MERCENARY**	0-515-09535-4 — $2.95
_Casca #2: **GOD OF DEATH**	0-515-09919-8 — $2.95
_Casca #3: **THE WAR LORD**	0-515-09996-1 — $2.95
_Casca #4: **PANZER SOLDIER**	0-515-09472-2 — $2.95
_Casca #5: **THE BARBARIANS**	0-515-09147-2 — $2.95
_Casca #6: **THE PERSIAN**	0-441-09264-0 — $2.95
_Casca #7: **THE DAMNED**	0-515-09473-0 — $2.95
_Casca #8: **SOLDIER OF FORTUNE**	0-515-09723-3 — $2.95
_Casca #9: **THE SENTINEL**	0-515-09997-X — $2.95
_Casca #10: **THE CONQUISTADOR**	0-515-09601-6 — $2.95
_Casca #11: **THE LEGIONAIRE**	0-515-09602-4 — $2.95
_Casca #12: **THE AFRICAN MERCENARY**	0-515-09474-9 — $2.95
_Casca #13: **THE ASSASSIN**	0-515-09911-2 — $2.95
_Casca #14: **THE PHOENIX**	0-515-09471-4 — $2.95
_Casca #15: **THE PIRATE**	0-515-09599-0 — $2.95
_Casca #16: **DESERT MERCENARY**	0-515-09556-7 — $2.95
_Casca #17: **THE WARRIOR**	0-515-09603-2 — $2.95
_Casca #18: **THE CURSED**	0-515-09109-X — $2.95
_Casca #19: **THE SAMURAI**	0-515-09516-8 — $2.95

Please send the titles I've checked above. Mail orders to:

BERKLEY PUBLISHING GROUP
390 Murray Hill Pkwy., Dept. B
East Rutherford, NJ 07073

NAME _____

ADDRESS _____

CITY _____

STATE _____ ZIP _____

Please allow 6 weeks for delivery.
Prices are subject to change without notice.

POSTAGE & HANDLING:
$1.00 for one book, $.25 for each additional. Do not exceed $3.50.

BOOK TOTAL	$_____
SHIPPING & HANDLING	$_____
APPLICABLE SALES TAX (CA, NJ, NY, PA)	$_____
TOTAL AMOUNT DUE	$_____

PAYABLE IN US FUNDS.
(No cash orders accepted.)

Their mission began the day the world ended...

THE GUARDIANS
by Richard Austin

The Guardians, the elite four-man
survival team. Fighting off bands of marauding
criminals, Russian spies, and whatever
else the postnuclear holocaust may bring,
the Guardians battle for freedom's last hope.

__ **THE GUARDIANS**	0-515-09069-7/$2.95
__ **TRIAL BY FIRE**	0-515-09070-0/$2.95
__ **THUNDER OF HELL**	0-515-09034-4/$2.95
__ **NIGHT OF THE PHOENIX**	0-515-09035-2/$2.95
__ **ARMAGEDDON RUN**	0-515-09036-0/$2.95
__ **WAR ZONE**	0-515-09273-8/$2.95
__ **BRUTE FORCE**	0-515-08836-6/$2.95
__ **DESOLATION ROAD**	0-515-09004-2/$2.95
__ **VENGEANCE DAY**	0-515-09321-1/$2.95

Please send the titles I've checked above. Mail orders to:

BERKLEY PUBLISHING GROUP
390 Murray Hill Pkwy., Dept. B
East Rutherford, NJ 07073

NAME_____

ADDRESS_____

CITY_____

STATE_____ZIP_____

Please allow 6 weeks for delivery.
Prices are subject to change without notice.

POSTAGE & HANDLING:
$1.00 for one book, $.25 for each
additional. Do not exceed $3.50.

BOOK TOTAL	$_____
SHIPPING & HANDLING	$_____
APPLICABLE SALES TAX (CA, NJ, NY, PA)	$_____
TOTAL AMOUNT DUE	$_____

PAYABLE IN US FUNDS.
(No cash orders accepted.)